MW00774793

# FLAME

### GALAXY ALIEN MAIL ORDER BRIDES: A QURILIXEN WORLD NOVELLA

## MICHELLE M. PILLOW

MICHELLE M. PILLOW® - MICHELLEPILLOW.COM

Galaxy Alien Mail Order Brides: Flame

© Copyright 2016 - 2018, Michelle M. Pillow

Second Printing July 2018

First Printing October 2016

Published by The Raven Books LLC

ISBN 978-1-62501-289-0

ALL RIGHTS RESERVED.

**This book or any portion thereof may not be reproduced or used in any manner whatsoever without the express written permission of the publisher except for the use of brief quotations in a book review.**

This novel is a work of fiction. Any and all characters, events, and places are of the author's imagination and should not be confused with fact. Any resemblance to persons, living or dead, or events or places is merely coincidence.

*Michelle M. Pillow*® is a registered trademark of The Raven Books LLC

## ABOUT THE BOOK

### FLAME

Vin (aka Flame) can't believe he's in yet another holding cell. Stupid Earthlings wouldn't know fun if it bit them in the hindquarters. Speaking of fun, the hot little number who claims she's a guard at the jail has been making his body respond in ways he's very happy about. If only she'd get on board with the plan and help him escape back to his ship. First she'd have to believe he's an alien. Right now she's taken to thinking he's crazy.

GALAXY ALIEN MAIL ORDER
BRIDES SERIES

Spark
Flame
Blaze
Ice
Frost
Snow

The Playful Prince
The Bound Prince
The Rogue Prince
The Pirate Prince

## Captured by a Dragon-Shifter Series

Determined Prince
Rebellious Prince
Stranded with the Cajun
Hunted by the Dragon
Mischievous Prince
Headstrong Prince

## Space Lords Series

His Frost Maiden
His Fire Maiden
His Metal Maiden
His Earth Maiden
His Woodland Maiden

**Dynasty Lords Series**
Seduction of the Phoenix
Temptation of the Butterfly

To learn more about the Qurilixen World series of
books and to stay up to date on the latest book list
visit www.MichellePillow.com

AUTHOR UPDATES

To stay informed about when a new book in the
series installments is released, sign up for updates:

michellepillow.com/author-updates

# WELCOME TO GALAXY BRIDES

## A NOTE FROM THE AUTHOR

Dear Readers,

For those of you familiar with my bestselling series, Dragon Lords, you've already been introduced to the Galaxy Brides Corporation and the services they offer lonely men and women of the future. What you might not have known is that Galaxy Brides (formerly aka "Galaxy Alien Mail Order Brides") dabbled in taking grooms to destinations—namely Earth! Unfortunately, they found the alien males a little too hard to control once they landed on our surface.

I hope you have as much fun reading this series as I've had writing it!

Happy Reading!

Michelle M. Pillow

*To My Awesome Husband, John*

## HOOVER DAM AIRSPACE, NEVADA-ARIZONA BORDER, UNITED STATES OF AMERICA, PLANET EARTH

Earth women better watch out. Vinglarkenbauer was on the prowl.

Wait, no. His Earth name was Flame. He really needed to remember that. Otherwise, he might not blend in with the humans, and they would suspect he was an extraterrestrial.

Earth women better watch out. Flame was on the prowl.

"As we begin our quiet descent into Earth's airspace, we are required to remind you to exercise caution while on world. Earth humans are not aware of alien life outside of their own. Informing them of it, or providing proof, is in direct violation of Federation law and your contracts. If questioned, please remember your onboard training," the now familiar intercom voice instructed.

Vin grinned as the Galaxy Alien Mail Order Brides' luxury shuttlecraft brought him closer to their vacation destination. Well, technically, this was a matchmaking journey to find a bride. Their cousin, Kal, had used Vin's and his brother Sev's thumbprints to sign a contract on their behalves while they were passed out after a Summer Setting celebration.

"Your Earth identification, local currency, and emergency retrieval button will be in your debarkation kit," the announcement continued. Vin had never seen the man's face, but his voice was a constant stream during the entire flight. "Please take a moment to memorize your credentials and to ensure the Earth name you chose upon contract signing is the same."

"They treat us like idiots," Sev, his brother, grumbled under his breath. "We get it. Don't tell people we're aliens. They'll panic."

"The only exception is any female you choose to mate," Vin spoke along with the voice. He'd memorized this part of the announcement since the Galaxy Bride people only explained it daily during the trip.

"All necessary papers will be filed for your new mate when you leave the planet."

Vin strapped himself into the chair next to Sev. "Where's Kal?"

"Probably signing us up to be fathers," Sev grumbled, as he closed his eyes. "Why not force us to procreate? He already signed us up to be married."

"Give our cousin a break. Kal's intentions were decent enough," Vin said. "And you heard him. We just have to pretend to look. We don't have to actually find a bride."

Vin ignored his brother's surly behavior. Sev always meant well, but he carried the heavy weight of responsibility on his shoulders. Their parents had died when one of the mine's air locks malfunctioned. The heat from Bravon's surface had rolled in, instantly cooking those in its path. Death had been swift, and there had been nothing to place on the surface funeral pyres. Vin had been old enough to care for himself according to Killian custom, but Sev took on the role of parent anyway, always worrying.

Going to a new planet, or really *any* planet that wasn't their fireball of a homeworld, Bravon, always held some appeal. Unfortunately, this trip was tainted by the fact their cousin had signed them up to be grooms in exchange for a discounted trip. Galaxy

Brides needed to prove that Earth women were compatible to alien men, but not many men wanted to venture to such a remote location.

Vin wasn't as upset as Sev was about it, but he wasn't eager to be given a deadline to find a wife.

Galaxy Alien Mail Order Brides was a relatively new corporation with the goal of exploiting the need most humanoids had for companionship. In the Killian humanoids' case, they were lonely ash miners living in the underground settlement of Frxsolis located in the Solarus Quadrant. They had very little by way of dating options, let alone marriage. His people had a roughness the rest of the universes lacked, so they certainly didn't get many visitors. The Killian people's tough personalities couldn't take all the credit. The surface temperature of their world reached over seven thousand degrees during the one month of summer and trapped them underneath the ground in the mines. The other months were a little better. Ships with the proper solar protectant could land for only short periods of time.

Kal thought it was hilarious to have stolen their thumbprints signatures while they were passed out after a celebration. And, since they'd willing walked onto the spaceship for what they thought was a luxury vacation, it would be hard convincing any legal entity that they had been duped.

So, here they were, landing on a primitive planet in search of a wife.

Searching didn't mean finding.

Vin would play along. He'd explore. He'd try to make sure his older brother didn't have too bad of a time, and his cousin... The truth was, Sev had contemplated leaving Kal on the blue floating orb. So Vin would try to make sure his cousin made it back onto the ship when they left.

"Why are you smiling?" Kal's voice interrupted his thoughts as he joined them. Vin glanced over to see his cousin eyeing Sev. Kal took his seat to prepare for landing. "You're coming around, aren't you? Someone's excited to be landing in a sea of females."

"Someone is imagining your face as I disengage the airlock into deep space," Sev answered without opening his eyes to return Kal's look.

A nearby passenger gasped as if horrified by what Sev had said. Vin leaned forward in his chair. It was only one of the guys from the Werten fuel docks. He wasn't sure what the alien's lineage was, but the man was slender and looked a little sickly, or maybe he had never seen hard labor.

"I almost feel sorry for the Earth woman," Vin

said. Apparently, ancient humans on Earth had recurrent contact with alien visitors and became blended with many alien races. They then, for the most part, forgot about aliens being real. Being remote and isolated, Earth became a unique location. It had all the sexual compatibility a virile male would need with none of the intergalactic politics.

"Not everyone on this ship can be a Killian god." Kal flexed his arms in the way shown on the Earth videos. They wore Earth clothing—tight denim pants, and gray t-shirts. During training, they were allowed to choose their style. All three of them picked the workingman attire without question. Sickly Werten man had gone for the rich businessman look.

There were a few with strange sparkly jumpsuits and pompadour hairstyles. That group declared themselves royalty and did a lip curl and hip shake in the middle of conversations. Vin avoided them.

"I don't feel right about this," Sev stated, not for the first time. "Earth is too remote and too primitive. We should not disembark. It is not too late to go somewhere else."

"Go where? Vin is banned from the Larceny Casino ships. We can't afford the trip to Quazer, let alone Quazer itself," Kal stated.

"I hear the industrial smog stacks on Rayvik are breath-stealing this time of year," Vin offered with a smirk. "Literally."

"They might be better than the humans we watched on the rogue transmission waves," Sev quipped. "I do not trust the images Galaxy Brides shows us. The humans are too happy."

"Maybe there is something in their food supply, or water, or air that makes them happy?" Vin offered.

"They claim the food and air in this Las Vegas sector of Nevada in the territory of the United States is safe for our biology," Vin said.

"Perhaps we will be happy after we ingest it as well?" Kal suggested. Then, to Vin, he added, "And I believe you only have to call it Las Vegas, not the Las Vegas sector of Nevada in the territory of the United States."

"Want to know what is safe for our biology?" Vin grinned. "The ladies. Oh, yeah, the sexy, fiery ladies. I'm going to find one of those sparkly ones with the giant feather headdresses."

"You have to admit, the personal droids in the suites were nice," Kal persisted. "And the ship has been first class the entire way. When else will we have the chance to enjoy luxury like this again?"

Sev grumbled an answer but nodded. "Sure, but the uploads weren't enjoyable."

"We had to learn the language and culture somehow," Vin said. "A small price."

"Stop finding excuses to be unhappy," Kal said.

"As we begin our final descent," the intercom voice resumed, "please check to make sure you have your travel kits with you including your identification modules and Earth currency. Droids will be checking costumes as you leave to ensure everything is in order. And, again, we must remind you, anyone attempting to bring non-Earth contraband onto the planet will be severely fined. This includes Letame taming orbs, nef vials, Datlis harnesses..."

As the man continued to list contraband items, Vin reached into the duffel bag they'd given him and pulled out his ID card. It read, "Flame Glarken." Sev was named Blaze, and Kal was now Spark.

Flame, Blaze, and Spark. Kal assured them that he had chosen tough, manly names for the planet. He had shown them an image of Earth women worshipping men with such names by sticking pieces of paper down their tiny hip coverings. Vin didn't currently wear the hip coverings under his jeans. He found them to be too constrictive.

"Due to the dense population and constant

activity of the area we will be taking you to, emergency pick up could be slightly delayed in some sectors," intercom man continued. "Please utilize the transmitters in your luggage the moment you encounter anything worrisome. We would rather have false alarms than an escalated situation. Should you find yourself in an escalated situation first try to remove yourself from the area. If you cannot remove yourself from the situation, do not panic."

"Escalated situations?" Sev inserted with a snort of disgust. "Why would we call for help? If a Killian can't take on an Earthling and win, then we deserve to be left behind to rot."

"That's the best thing I've heard them mention so far," Vin agreed. "I could use a good brawl."

What Sev hadn't been told was that Earth dangers weren't just from Earthlings. Kal had confided in Vin that he'd heard some rumors on the back channel communication forums about the abduction of unsuspecting aliens by space pirates, who then sold them for secret Earth government studies in exchange for valuable planetary resources. Then there were reports alluding to cloning black markets where a healthy alien specimen were experimented on and studied like lab rats in a cage, which then led to the creation of something called a savant

—a half human half alien hybrid—used by Earth's organized crime families to track alien life forms. Though crude, it was an effective way of hunting offworlders trying to blend in. However, all of these were unfounded space gossip, nothing more. If he were to ask those same people about the Killian male, he'd hear warnings of alien flesh-eating and ritual sun sacrifices—none of which were true.

"Try to remember there is no galactic traffic here," Sev warned. "If this blister popping operation can't get us out of trouble, we're going to be trapped. It's best to keep mischief to a minimum."

"I thought you said we could take the Earthlings in a fight," Vin teased. "Which is it? Can we win, or are you scared of them?"

"Do not make me solder your lips together," Sev answered. Vin knew his brother prided himself on his fighting skills. They all did.

"Focus on the ladies," Kal said with a dreamy smile. "The sparkly, soft, pliable ladies who will all want us."

Vin smiled as the ship angled slightly. Kal slid in his seat. It was enough to shut his cousin up.

"It is important to remember to inform your group where you are at all times," the voice instructed. "Should something happen, they will be able to contact the Galaxy Alien Mail Order Brides ship on your behalf. If the local authorities arrest you, say nothing. We monitor all channels and will come for you. This trip is designed to ensure optimal mating opportunities for everyone. Please enjoy yourselves and be safe. Thank you for joining us on our maiden Earth voyage, and for choosing Galaxy Alien Mail Order Brides where we join hearts across the universes."

A holographic image of Earth appeared before them, showing their landing destination on the abnormally blue planet. By comparison, their home-world of Bravon was an ashen, gray, desolate land-scape with no surface water.

The possibilities were endless for an entrepreneurial guy whose aim was to retire before the ash of the Bravon mines killed him. The average age expectancy on his home planet was frighten-ingly low. So low, no one discussed it. Besides, it wasn't the Killian way to complain. Life was much better for those who didn't work the mines, and in order for that to happen, Vin needed something he could sell.

Killians loved three things—food, drink, and a good fight.

Vin wanted more. He'd seen several of the elders

end up as invalids, and his own parents had been melted in a heat blast.

*Focus on finding an idea to take back home...* he thought to himself.

"I don't know why these Galaxy Brides guys are so worried," Vin said as he stretched his neck muscles. "I'm sure we'll blend in with the natives just fine. How hard can it be?"

.

## 2

LAS VEGAS, NEVADA, UNITED STATES OF
AMERICA, PLANET EARTH

*ONE WEEK LATER...*

"Give me all your Funky Chunky Cho Chocolate and your Vanilla Surprise. I don't know what the
surprise is, but I like the color spots in it. Not spots.
Sprinkles. Spotty sprinkles."

Vin's hands shook as he pointed down to the ice
cream buckets hidden by a glass case. His breathing
deepened in anticipation. He'd been searching up
and down the Las Vegas strip for it and finally found
an ice cream stand hidden inside a giant casino's
shopping center. Soft lighting, giant statues, and the
indoor glass lakes held no appeal for him. He wanted
the ice cream. He needed it. The shaking became
worse as he gripped the top of the counter.

"Now, give it to me, now," he insisted when the girl behind the counter only stared at him with widened eyes. "And the pink one. Give me the pink one. Hurry. Now!"

Vin snorted deep and then wiped his nose with the back of his hand. It caused the girl behind the counter to wrinkle her expression as she frowned at him.

"Uh, Brett?" the girl whispered helplessly. Had she forgotten how to do her job? Seriously, how hard was it to hand him a bucket and a spoon? Couldn't she see he needed it?

"No. I am not Brett. I am called Flame. I'll need a spoon," he muttered, tapping the case. "Hurry, hurry, now, now, now..."

"Ok, sir, just calm down." A young man with a "Brett" name tag appeared. He held up his hands and gestured as if he expected Vin to bow his head to receive a special ice cream blessing.

Vin grimaced and lowered his head while keeping his eyes on Brett and the employee who apparently couldn't understand how to take a simple food order. A green-colored ice cream caught his attention. "I'll take the green bucket, too."

When Brett only continued with his strange

hand gestures, Vin lifted his head and said. "I can do it myself."

He stormed around the ice cream counter and slid the case's access panel open. The girl gasped and scurried away from him. Brett was slower to back up as if protecting the girl.

Vin ignored them both as he grabbed a scoop from inside a bucket and brought a to his lips. A strange chorus of noises rose up around him, but he didn't care. Earth people were so noisy, and he chose to block the voices out.

The cold, smooth flavor passed his lips, and he groaned as the shaking began to ease. He took another scoop, and then another, licking and swallowing the sweet, sweet, precious morsels. First pink, then white, then brown, then green, then white with brown specks, then...

"Sir, we're going to need you to step away from the case," a woman ordered, interrupting his flow.

*Scorched blistersack!*

Where was he? Now he needed to start over. He reached his hand in, using his fingers instead of the scoop. The natural warmth of his body caused the ice cream to melt, so he needed to bring it to his lips fast.

First pink, then white, then brown, then green...

"Sir, put the ice cream down," the woman

demanded, louder than before. "Back away from the ice cream."

*Fiery crevices!*

First pink, then white, then...

"Sir!"

*Fire balls!*

A hand tentatively touched his arm, and he shrugged it off. First pink, then...

"Careful, Borden," a man warned. "Maybe I should—"

"It's all right, Officer Harris," the woman answered soothingly. Her tone remained calm as if talking to a rampaging Egrat mammoth. "We're just talking. Sir, have you taken any drugs today? What are you on, sir? I need you to look at me, please."

The hand touched him again. The shaking in his limbs had subsided, and his head felt better. He pulled is fingers from a bucket. White dripped onto the floor as the ice cream melted. He turned to face the woman.

Brown eyes met his, and he found it hard to breathe. His heartbeat quickened. She wore her hair pulled back from her face, the style clean and neat and very unlike the other women he'd seen walking around Vegas. She had the kind of lips that would light up her entire face if she was to smile at him.

"Sir, I need you to put the weapon down." The beauty looked stern.

Blast. No smile.

He angled his fingers toward the floor, and the clump of ice cream fell off them. Vin grinned and felt a small trail of ice cream move down his chin. How had he not heard the sultry tone of her voice before now?

"Sir?" She reached for his hand, and he lifted his fingers so she could take it. Instead of clasping her hand around his, she slowly removed the ice cream scoop he held and dropped it aside. "There you go."

"You're lovely," Vin said, smiling wider. The words were breathless. Tiny jolts of excitement filtered through him.

"You're going to have to come with us," Harris stated. He wore a similar uniform as Vin's dream woman.

Vin arched the brow at the man. He did not wish to go anywhere with him. The woman, however…

"Can you come with us?" she asked.

"Of course." Vin smiled. He'd follow her wherever she wanted.

"What's your name?" she continued, her tone pleasant in its calmness.

"My name is Vinglarkenbauer. I mean Flame.

17

Not Vinglarkenbauer. Just Flame. What is your name?"

"Borden?" Harris asked. Vin really wished the man would quit interrupting. He was finally getting somewhere talking to a pretty Earth woman, and this idiot was going to ruin his chances of a date.

"We're just talking, Harris," Borden answered. She reached behind her toward the man. "Hand me your cuffs."

Harris began mumbling something about how Vin had the right not to talk if he didn't want to talk, and how he could go to a tourney, whether he could pay for it or not. He'd seen signs for a medieval show jousting tourney. If that is what this woman wanted to do with him, he'd go and happily. Finally, Harris finished his interruption with, "Do you understand these rights?"

"Borden." Vin made a move to touch her face. "That is a beautiful name."

She leaned away from his hand. "It's Angela. Hold your hands out in front of you, please, Mr. Flame."

"Do you understand," Harris repeated.

"Yes. Fine. However I wish to talk to her, not you." Vin glanced at Harris and obeyed Angela's request as he held out his hands for her. "This man called you Borden, Angela."

"Holy shit, you're the crazy whisperer," Harris muttered.

"Angela Borden." Angela wrapped a metal band around his wrist. "You may call me Angela."

Vin glanced down at the present. "Thank you. It's lovely."

"Yes," Angela agreed. She snapped a second metal band around his other wrist, linking them together. "There we are. Now, I'll need you to come with us."

"Do we have to go with him? It could just be the two of us." Vin couldn't take his eyes off her. Every detail of her mesmerized his senses. To be fair, the quick beating of his heart could have been from the ice cream sugar, but he knew for a fact the rest of his reactions were all from her. He shifted his hips. Yes, the erection was all for her. Should he tell her that? A woman had told his cousin Kal that honesty was important. He opened his mouth to let her know how much he wanted her when she again spoke.

"I'm sorry. I can't leave my chaperone behind," she said. "Officer Harris has to come."

"I understand. I have heard of this custom for the

sake of virtue. A woman as beautiful as you would have many suitors. It is wise you take protection in such a crowd. Yes, I would be honored to join you," Vin agreed. Then, to Brett, he instructed, "Please have the buckets delivered to my room and charge my suite."

Brett looked confused.

"Officer Harris is going to have to pat you down," Angela said. "Just to make sure you don't have any sharp objects or weapons on your person."

"I do not have any weapons on me." Vin gave her a small smile and winked. Women liked when a man had humor. He thought about making a joke about the weapon between his legs, but Harris began touching him, and Vin grimaced instead. Luckily the check was over quickly, and the man retreated. Instead, he went with, "Unless you count my fists in a fight."

"He's clean. No ID," Harris said.

"Well, you just keep those fists to yourself and we won't have any problems." Angela grabbed a stack of napkins and held them in from of his face. "Is it all right if I clean you up?"

Vin nodded in agreement.

"You don't have to do that," Harris stated.

"It's fine," Angela said. "Nothing wrong with a little human dignity."

"We'll talk again after you've been accepted onto the force and worked the strip for a few years," Harris answered.

"I've lived in this area my whole life," Angela countered. "I don't think there is any brand of crazy I haven't already seen."

"Let's just see if you make it on, and then we'll talk," Harris said.

"I'll make it. They'll take me because you're going to give me a good recommendation when this is over, aren't you, Officer Harris? And the department wants you to recruit more women." Angela gently wiped the napkins on his sticky chin, trying to clean the ice cream that had trailed down it. Vin didn't lose his smile. "There you go. That's better, Mr. Flame."

"Thank you." He began to lean in for a kiss, but she stepped back too quickly and tossed the napkins on the nearby counter. As Angela strolled with him through the shopping center, he ignored the fact Harris escorted them on their impromptu date. "I am fascinated by all the shops you have here. They sell everything. One had nothing but tiny little cups they called shot glasses for when you only want a tiny shot of water and not a full drink. Fascinating, isn't it? And another store sold nothing but t-shirts. I bought this one, do you like it?" He pointed to the beer label printed on his chest. "Apparently, it is stylish because this is the only design they had. And another sold these bath bombs that you throw into the water and watch fizz. I put it in the toilet in the hotel bathroom, and it made strange pink bubbles. I'm not sure why someone would need a store for that, but apparently, they are very popular."

"Yes, sir, there are a lot of businesses," Angela answered.

"I thought about opening a business back home," Vin admitted, not sure what prompted him to tell this woman his deepest dreams. "Maybe an ice cream business. But I am not sure the weather would permit. Storage will be a problem. And then there is the exporting of ingredients. We don't have sugar. I like sugar."

"I can tell." Angela smirked as if trying not to laugh.

"Would you enjoy some? I am having it brought to my suite. You're welcome to join me," Vin offered.

Harris gave a small laugh. "Looks like you got an admirer."

"Where?" Vin frowned, glancing around the area. All around him, toxins were being emitted. He tried to block them. Earth had a lot of smells and noises. The machines and fluorescent lights gave off a chemical smell that none of the locals seemed to notice, and the casinos were filled with billows of smoke from tiny sticks people put in their mouths. It didn't take the skill of a Killian nose to analyze that those things were not healthy to ingest into a biological system, but that didn't stop the humans from firing up one after another.

Sometimes, Vin could detect the cancer inside of their bodies killing them. The one man he'd tried to tell that to had become violently angry. The old guy yelled about his God-given human right to smoke any damned thing he so chose without having to listen to hippy liberals and their agendas. Vin supposed the man was right. It was his decision if he wanted to die from the cancer in the next two years instead of seeking medical help.

The visual stimulus for Vin wasn't so much in the aesthetic like it was for Kal, but in how he *felt* about things. It was more of an impression, a combination of sounds and nearly invisible imprints emitting from the various machines—slot machines on the casino floor, phones in people's pockets, cash registers, and card readers. Every time someone won at one of the machines, or answered their cellular phone, or paid with a credit card, the intensity of the impressions became unbearable to look directly at.

Several people watched them as they walk by. He focused his attention on the men. Which one was his competition for Angela's attention? He held up his hands so they could see the joined bracelets she'd given him. Several gave him strange looks, and he could only assume they were jealous.

"Through here," Angela ordered, taking him toward a door marked security. She pulled a card from her pocket and slid it through a scanner. The door led to a private hallway, and he relaxed. No competition in here. Just Harris the chaperone.

Vin relaxed and kept talking. "There is not much call for a shirt with only one label on it, at least not a whole store full. Food would be something, but everyone eats in the settlement dining hall together, so I'm not sure how I could get them to change locations since food production is communal."

"You could always deliver the food, or have a food truck," Angela suggested. "Sometimes people don't want to have to get dressed and go out to eat. You could bring the food to them."

Vin thought about her idea for a long moment before slowly nodding. "You may be right. Start a delivery service that brings food to the people. There might be something to that."

"Glad I could help," Angela answered. "Now, if

you wouldn't mind helping me out by stepping into my office?"

"Yes, Angela, I'd be happy to help you in any way you needed." Vin grinned, moving through the door she held open.

"You may sit here," she gestured to a bench surrounded by bars.

He stepped into the small enclosure and looked around at the bars. "This is what you call a zoo theme, correct? The decorating you do in these rooms is amazing."

"Yep, buddy, and you're the lion on display," Harris answered as he shut the door and clicked the lock.

"I'm not a lion, I'm human," Vin corrected.

"My mistake," Harris answered. To Angela, he said, "All right, trainee, well done. Time to do your paperwork."

"Hand me the cuff keys." She held out her hand to Harris. He dug in his pocket. To Vin, she said. "Slide your hands through the bar, and I'll get those off you."

Vin looked at his wrists. "I would rather keep them if that's all right. You gave them to me, and they are lovely. I'm sorry if I wasn't appreciative enough."

Harris stopped digging in his pocket. "Suit yourself."

"Any chance I can convince you to do the logs for me?" Angela asked Harris. A phone began to ring, and they both ignored it.

"Nice try," Harris laughed. "This one is all you, darling."

"Would you like me to pick that device up and speak?" Vin offered, not liking the noise. They didn't answer him.

"I don't even know what we can charge him with, really," Angela said to her friend. "He offered to pay for the food he ate when he was finished. He didn't resist arrest. He does not appear to be drunk, but he may be on something. Public disturbance, a misdemeanor?"

A voice began talking from the little box on Harris' shoulder. Vin couldn't make out much from the garbled dialect, but the man's expression became serious.

"It's all hands on deck. I have to go. There was some kind of pile-up accident on the strip. Traffic is backed up, and half the force went to secure the scene. Also, a fight broke out on a casino floor between a couple of jackass kids, and there are reports of a possible robbery attempt. Just another night in Vegas. Stay here until I get back. Just write the report up the best you can, and I'll sign it later," Harris instructed.

"Do you need me to come?" Angela offered.

"Sorry, but you're stuck babysitting him until things get cleared up. You going to be all right on your own?"

Angela looked up at the clock. "Yeah, I'm good. The receptionist will be back from her break soon to man the phones. I won't be alone for too long."

Harris made his way toward the door. "We'll probably have to call in a psych request for this one. Something here isn't right."

"On it," Angela acknowledged, taking a seat behind a computer.

Vin cringed at how the radiation from the computer screen stuck to Angela's clothing. Earth technology could really use an advancement. He had seen images of the older systems and had done the calculations of radiation as a youngster. The systems had been replaced eons ago on Bravon and other planets mainly due to the health hazards they presented. If he had his guess, some alien race had sold the secret Earth government group the old technology. The humans should have held out for safer, but then, they didn't know any better, and now the same aliens would be able to sell them progressively enhanced technology each time they came.

The radiation was a natural concern for him if any of them were to actually find brides to take home, especially if they were to have children later.

"You are quite fond of your clunky processors here, aren't you?" Vin smiled, trying to rekindle the conversation and draw her eyes away from the screen back to him. Now that they were alone, they could speak more openly about the clear attraction building between them. He glanced at her thighs, seeing what could only be the faint trace of desire waving in the air like heat.

"Excuse me?" Angela looked up from what she was doing.

"Your computers emit more radiation than they're worth. I could calculate the probability of most things in less time it takes you to enter the data into that thing. All the while, it's killing you."

"Ah, ok then. Thank you for that tip. I'll write you down as a technophobe," she said.

Vin smiled, happy to know he was making a good impression on her.

## 3

ANGELA TRIED NOT to look at the man sitting in the temporary holding cell as she wrote up her report. There was something about him, beyond the fact he was the first man she'd ever handcuffed while on the job. She'd been given basic training provided by Metro police before being allowed into the J.O.R.S. pilot program, *Junior Officer Recruitment Search.* As a push to strengthen their numbers, it had been decided to recruit from within the ranks of casino security. Security officers knew Vegas, knew casino policy, proved they weren't afraid of confrontation, and the program hoped to build upon the relationship between the major casinos and the police force.

"All right, Mr. Flame." Angela dared a glance in his direction. This might be a strange case to start whatever future career this program might lead to, but she was going to do everything perfectly and show the bosses that she could be trusted to handle her business no matter how bizarre things became. And in Vegas, bizarre was something they had an abundance of. Talking as she typed, she said, "Hair, brown. Sex, male. Height, approximately seven feet. Eyes..." She studied his face. "Metallic contacts? Are your eyes brown?"

"They are my eyes," he said.

"Eyes, brown," Angela said as she typed. "So, care to tell me why you decided it was a good idea to push your way behind the ice cream counter and help yourself?"

"Sure." Flame grinned, standing as she addressed him. He moved in front of the bars, and she was glad they were there as they kept him from coming too close to her.

When she'd touched him, the heat from his body radiated down her fingers and into her stomach. The adrenaline from her first real call under the watchful gaze of Officer Harris could attribute a little to the reaction, but she'd be an idiot not to recognize the attraction for what it was. This Vinglarken-Flame was definitely a person of interest.

*Oh, great, now my fantasies are starting to sound like cop talk.*

Angela took a deep breath, attempting to center herself and concentrate on the task at hand. A tiny bit of napkin where she'd tried to wipe off his face clung to his beard. A black tribal tattoo appeared from beneath his right neckline and also from beneath the sleeve. Now that the situation was calmer, she found herself looking at his chest. It was nothing but muscle. What the hell had she been thinking, approaching a man like that? One smack and he could have ended her life.

Oh, but there was something virile about a man like this—sexy, strong, powerful, confident.

*This is going to look great on your record,* she assured herself. *Well, done, Ang. You handled yourself like a pro and got him in without incident.*

*Don't you mean luck, you dumbass?* Herself seemed to mock back. *What the hell are you doing playing cop? Flame? Sounds like a biker name if I ever heard one. His buddies are probably going to come looking for you now.*

*I need this promotion. I need this raise. I need to get my mom out of that place and into somewhere that can provide her with the therapies she needs.*

The reminder of her mother steeled her resolve,

and she shook all thoughts of desire out of her mind. When he didn't elaborate, she prompted, "So, why did you decide it was a good idea to push your way behind the ice cream counter and help yourself?"

Angela held her hands over the keyboard and prepared to type his answer.

"I needed it," Flame said.

"Needed ice cream? How so?"

"I'm having a period. I was craving sugar."

Angela automatically began to type, *I'm having a period. I was craving...*

As his answer sunk in, she stopped with a surprised laugh before regaining her composure. So, Mr. Flame wasn't going to take this seriously. "You are having your period?"

"Yes." He looked completely serious. "I am."

*Multiple personality disorder? Wait, no, they call it something else now. Dis. Dis. Dis-something. Shit, I know this.*

The door opened and Mags, the night receptionist, entered. She blinked in surprise as Angela lifted her hand in greeting.

"I see we have a guest." Mags had been working for the casinos for so long the lifestyle seemed to seep out of her wrinkled pores. Her smoky breath reeked of the years spent on the casino floor. Her short skirts and black pantyhose called to her youth as a waitress and a cigarette girl, and her over-sprayed hair appeared as if its style hadn't changed since the 1950s when she'd attended her last Elvis concert.

"Mags, meet Flame," Angela said, looking more at her computer than the two she introduced. She deleted the line about the period. Maybe with an audience, he'd give her a real answer. "Flames, this is Mags."

"Pleased to meet you, Mags," Flame said, completely polite.

"Likewise," Mags answered. When Angela glanced at the woman, she was placing her transparent red scarf on her desk. Mags smiled, reminding Angela of the stories the woman told from her years working as a bartender during the exotic male dance shows. It would seem age did not limit a woman's appreciation of the sexy male form. "What you in for?"

"Angela asked me to step in here," Flame answered.

Mags laughed. "That's quite an accent you have, there, Flame. Not from these parts, are you?"

"No. I am not," Flame agreed.

"Anyway," Angela stated to end Mags' flirting, even though she probably had no reason or right to be jealous of the woman getting the crazy man's attention. "You were saying, why did you decide it was a good idea to push your way behind the ice cream counter and help yourself?"

Mags laughed, and commented under her breath, "Been there."

"I told you, I was craving sugar because I'm on my period," Flame stated.

"Definitely been there," Mags put forth.

*Dissociative identity disorder. That's what they called it.*

"Are you currently undergoing sex change treatments?" Mags inquired as if she didn't understand her question could have been construed as rude. "Because from where I'm sitting you, sweetheart, look all man."

"Thank you," Flame said.

"You're a man," Angela insisted, trying to gauge his state of mind.

"Yes. I am," Flame answered. Dark eyes stayed steadily on her, slowly traveling up and down her body as if he could feel her with his gaze.

Angela shivered, fighting sexual awareness. "Men can't have periods."

"Not true. I have periods all the time," he countered. "We are having a period of time now."

"Oh, sweetheart, I think you got that lost in translation," Mags stated. "That is not what having a period means. It means your baby growing tunnel is shedding its inner lining and you're bleeding out of your—"

"All right, Mags, thank you," Angela interrupted the inappropriate description of menstruation. "I have an interview to conduct."

"Sorry, Officer Wet Blanket." Mags didn't sound at all upset. The phone began to ring again, and she reached for it. "You really aren't as much fun now that you've gone all official on us."

Mags picked up the phone and began her normal back and forth as she talked to the caller.

Angela took a deep breath. Mags was right. No, she wasn't as much fun since the nursing home raised their rates beyond what Angela could afford and moved her mother to a substandard facility. There was nothing fun at all about her life right now.

"Mr. Flame, if you insist on claiming to be part woman with a menstrual cycle as your defense, I'm afraid I'm going to have to order a psych eval."

"What is that?"

"A psychological evaluation," Angela stated. She stood from her desk and slowly approached him by the bars. She kept her voice down, trying to keep their conversation as private as possible in front of Mags. "It's where they determine your mental health and whether or not you are a danger to yourself or others. If they find you are, you could be detained in one of their facilities. Now, my gut tells me you're not crazy, but I need you to help me out here."

"What does it mean to be detained in a facility? Prison?" His smile finally faltered as if he realized the extent of the trouble he was in. "You are saying if I don't tell you the truth, you will have people put me in prison? My brother told me of the wax prison you have on the strip where they encase humans in wax in strange poses so they are unable to move, and the families come to visit and take pictures with the people they know."

Wax museums?

"Please, I need you to take this seriously," she insisted. "All I need is an honest answer. Right now I don't think the charges are so severe that you can't get away with just a slap on the wrist."

Mags hung up the phone. "Some guy is peeing in the fountain."

"Dispatch it to someone on the floor. I can't leave right now," Angela said.

"Aye-aye, captain." Mags' chair creaked as she moved to grab a walkie-talkie.

"Honesty? And then I can avoid the wax prison?"

"Yes." Angela nodded.

"What would you like to know?" He reached a hand forward through the bar but didn't get very far with the handcuffs still on his wrists.

"Let's start with your real name. It's not Flame, is it?" Angela studied his face. Normally she could tell when people were lying, as this man obviously was, but she couldn't read his expressions. He'd make a great poker player that was for sure.

"No." He seemed to contemplate his answer, before saying, "But I am not allowed to tell my true name to just anyone. I can only tell the woman I am to marry."

"I seem to have read something about certain cultures thinking it is bad luck to use a person's real name. I can't remember what, though. Is this a Native American tribal thing?"

"No. It is a contract," Flame answered.

"You good here?" Mags asked. "I need a coffee. Want one?"

"No, nothing for me," Angela said.

"How about you, stud? Coffee?" Mags offered.

"No. But I would like a chocolate ice cream cone, please," he said. Mags laughed as she left the room.

Angela tried not to respond, but she couldn't help the little half-laugh that escaped her. "I don't want to go against any religious doctrine or contract that you follow, but I do need a name for the system."

"You want my name?"

"Yes. I would like your name."

Flame grinned. "Vinglarkenbauer."

"Vin Glarken Bauer?" she repeated slowly.

"Yes."

"Thank you, Vin. Now we are getting somewhere."

Vin glanced up at the ceiling and wrapped his fingers around the bars. "We are moving? It does not feel like we're moving."

"You said you had a brother here in Vegas with you. What's his name? Would you like me to call him?" she offered. "Where are you staying?"

"Here he is called Blaze. I also have a cousin we call Spark. We are staying in a suite at the top of a big building. I can take you there."

"Do Blaze and Spark have real names as well?"

"Sevglarkenbauer and Kalglarkenbauer."

"Sev and Kal? See, this isn't so hard," Angela said.

"Will you let me out now?" Vin asked. "I am not having fun in here, and I would like to leave this room and go to my suite, please. I wish to make sure Brett brought my ice cream like I asked. I did not find him to be a very capable man."

"I'm sorry, I can't do that," she said.

"But you said if I told you the truth." Vin frowned. "And I no longer wish to be in here like a caged human. Let me out."

"I promise to do what I can to help you if you tell me the truth." Angela crossed her arms over her chest. "Now, what are you doing in Vegas? Business? Pleasure?"

"I seek pleasure. I am taking a break from work. I do not think the humans here know how to have real fun, but I won't let that stop me from enjoying things while I am here."

"Where do you call home? What do you do for work?"

He hesitated.

"Is English a second language? Do you need me to slow down or anything to make me easier to understand?" Angela didn't think that was the case, but she wanted to be thorough and do a good job.

"I understand English perfectly." Vin pulled his arms off the bars. "My people are Killian. We come from a planet called Bravon. It is in the Solarus Quadrant, but I do not think you will have knowledge of this space unless you are part of the secret Earth government group who knows of alien existence. Are you?"

Angela slowly shook her head and took a step back.

"There is one settlement on Bravon called Frxsolis. It is where I am from. I am supposed to say I am from Canada, but I am not. Bravon is not like Earth. The temperature there is not cold like Las Vegas. It is so hot that protective gear is needed to breach the surface and we rely on turbines to pull air and energy from above to the settlement below. Most people cannot take the harsh existence that is life there, but we are used to it. We import much of our supplies, and in return, we export the ash we mine from the underground shafts. Some alien cultures use it for medical purposes, others sell it to galactic tourists, and then there are those who believe that the ash brings significant luck to the bearer because of its rarity and they use it in religious ceremonies. As I said before, I wish to start a new way of life and get out of the mines. Life expectancy in the tunnels is low. My parents died from a heat blast when there was a malfunction in—"

"Stop," Angela interrupted. "Please. Just stop talking."

"You asked for the truth."

"I, ah, yeah." Angela took another step back. She had so wanted him to be normal. She could allow herself to be secretly attracted to normal. "I did. And now I'm going to ask you to stop. You make yourself comfortable. I'm going to call a professional to come and talk to you now."

"But you said if I told you the truth, you would not give me a psychological evaluation." Vin frowned. Had this woman lied to him? "I do not wish to be detained."

Vin contemplated using force to free himself from what he considered to be an unnecessary confinement. It wasn't his fault the ice cream workers couldn't fulfill a simple order. He remained seated. The allure of being so close to Angela made his will to flee futile. He realized the irony of being imprisoned by her was exactly what he wanted.

"I said I'd try to help you." Angela slowly reached for the phone on her desk. "If you tell me you think you're an alien, then I don't have a choice. The best way for me to help you is to contact the professionals."

## 4

VIN WATCHED Angela dig her fingers into the hair on the back her head as she pressed her forehead against the top of the desk. The strands at the back of her head were lighter than the top, an integrated progression of color he'd seen on several of the Earth women. But none of the women he had seen looked as beautiful as she did. She had been in that position for some time. An occasional sigh or mutter would sound, but she didn't look at him again.

Vin was disappointed. He really thought he could trust her. But she did not keep her word and instead left him locked in a cell. The idea of a wax prison did not settle easily within his mind, but he wasn't too worried. This wasn't the first planet that had tried to lock him up. He knew that his brother would find him and rescue him. That is what Sev always did.

"It shouldn't be too much longer now." Angela finally lifted her head to look at him. Her gaze moved over his face, down his neck and body, before making its way once more to meet his eyes. "Are you sure that you don't want to tell me you were joking? This is your last chance to tell me the truth. You're not really an extraterrestrial, are you?"

"You asked me for honesty, and I gave you honesty. It is you who didn't keep your word." Vin frowned.

"Very well then." She sighed heavily. "I wish you luck, Mr. Vin Glarkenbauer or Flame or whatever you wish to call yourself." Angela pushed up from the chair. She leaned over to look at a small monitor that showed a picture of the hallway. Several men approached. "This must be them."

Vin watched as she walked toward the door. He glanced at the monitor and chuckled, seeing his brother's stern face. Sev was mad as hell.

"Hey, guys," Angela said, pulling the door open to invite the men in.

Two short, stocky men entered. Their heads were a little too big to be considered normal for humans and the fact was barely hidden by the tightly pulled skin suits they wore over their alien forms. Their smooth, black haircuts consisted of the same length hair all the way around their heads. They wore silver uniforms that looked suspiciously close to the Galaxy Alien Mail Order Brides' logo color.

"I am Bob. This is Gary. We are here to acquire your prisoner," Bob said. He recognized him as one of the ship's intercom voices.

"You're from...?" Angela prompted.

"We have orders to acquire your prisoner, Flame Glarken." Gary rudely pushed past Angela and moved toward the cell. His long arms swung by his sides.

"Wait a minute," Angela protested. "I'm going to need some ID. You can't just..."

Her words trailed off when Sev stepped into the office. Her eyes flew to Vin, and he knew she understood what was happening. Sev fixed her with a hard stare, and she stumbled back.

"You are not authorized to keep him," Gary stated. "Open the cage."

"He's not in that much trouble," Angela said. "This is a mistake. You don't want to do this. He'll probably just get a slap on the wrist."

Sev turned his eyes to Vin in question. "Vin? They want to beat you?"

"They wish to give me a psychological evaluation and put me in detainment," Vin explained. "Get me out."

"That makes sense. I often believe you need evaluated for your psychological, but not by primitives." Sev turned to Angela and in his most intimidating tone demanded, "Release my brother."

"I can't do that," she said, shaking.

"Don't harm her," Vin said. "I like her. She's interesting."

"Very well." Sev relaxed his stance. "Step aside, woman."

Angela's hands fumbled as she pulled open a drawer on her desk and reached in. "I can't let you do this."

"Open it," Sev ordered.

Gary lifted his hands, and they began to glow with an eerie green light.

"What the," Angela shook as she held up a square-tipped gun, "hell are you?"

They ignored her question.

"I need you to step away from my prisoner," Angela stated. She tried to sound tough, but Vin heard the tremor in her words. Even so, he was impressed she remained functional. When he wanted to, Sev intimidated most people no matter the alien race.

"What are you?" she demanded.

The skin suit melted from Gary's hands as he touched the bars, revealing the tough yellow flesh underneath. The bars also began to glow, extending out from his fingers. The sound of a metal latch unhooked, and the door opened. Gary stepped aside. The skin suit hung from his wrists like tattered sleeves.

Vin instantly went toward Angela. "I am sorry to have to leave you. I did enjoy my time with you and hope to do it again very soon."

Angela's hands jerked when he came to close. Two prongs flew from the end of her gun into Vin's chest. He felt the tingle of electricity move through his body, tickling him. Waves moved the air around her hands as he saw the pattern her gun made on the environment around it like the rippling of water. The prongs began to itch, and he wrapped his hand around the cords to pull them out. The bracelets she'd given him restricted his movements, and he let his skin heat up so he could pull the metal apart. His wrists were no longer joined, but he kept the individual bracelets on.

Angela gasped. "How...? What...? How...?"

"Vin, come," Sev ordered. "We are being moved to a new hotel. This stunt of yours has caused an uproar."

"I can't move to a new room right now," Vin said. The need was growing inside of him again, and he wanted to stop the tremors before they became a full-blown need. "I had ice cream buckets sent to our current suite and I want to enjoy them first."

"Look at me." Sev frowned and grabbed Vin's face in his hands to force him to do just that. "Your temperature is low, and you smell differently." He moved Vin's head to one side and then the other in examination. "You are acting erratically. You are lucky the Galaxy Brides ship watches—"

"Galaxy Alien Mail Order Brides," Bob corrected. "They don't like it when you shorten the name. Something about customer clarity."

"That's only for employees," Gary instructed.

"But you said..." Bob protested.

"Now is not the time," Gary lifted his skinless hand. "What would you like us to do with this woman? Should we take her back to the ship as your bride?"

"Leave her," Sev ordered.

"I like her," Vin said. "She's pretty and smells like

flowers. I want her to make pretty babies if she doesn't have too much radiation."

Angela made a weak noise.

"What is wrong with you?" Sev demanded.

"I've seen this. He has overindulged in a local drug," Gary stated. "We warned you against the local street vendors."

"What did you ingest?" Bob demanded. "Cocaine? Marijuana? Crack? Speed? Angel dust? LSD? Peyote? I quite like the peyote myself." He glanced at Gary and cleared his throat. "I mean the word, of course, not the drug. Molly? Clarity? X? E? G? K? Zing? Bliss? Meow Meow? Iv—"

"Ice cream," Vin interrupted, not understanding anything else the little man said. "Can we get some?"

"Ice cream?" Gary frowned. "That is a new one."

"I thought you said the food on this planet was safe." Sev released his brother and turned on Gary and Bob.

"Ice cream the food?" Bob repeated as if clarifying what they were dealing with.

"If you recall from the contract you signed, there are some risks involved when visiting a new planet," Gary inserted.

"I'm going to kill Kal," Sev swore. "And I'm

coming after all of you if my brother ends up in the wax prison with the other frozen people."

"Hey there, beautiful." Vin waved his fingers at Angela.

She made a small squeaky noise.

"Want to come to my suite with us?" Vin offered. "I find you attractive and—"

"Now is not the time," Sev broke in.

"N-no." Angela shook her head. Her gaze kept wandering toward Gary's skinless hands.

"We will have this ice cream situation analyzed and will administer an antidote," Gary said. "For now, you should restrain him on a bed, so he does not ingest anything else. Definitely, don't let him have any more food. The Reticulans have studied this entire region, and we will have reports on the biological make up of this ice cream."

"I want a transport off this planet," Sev stated. "This is unacceptable. I'm done here."

"We should go," Bob ordered as he looked at the device on his wrist. "A lady enters the hallway."

Vin glanced at the monitor to see Mags carrying a cup of coffee and an ice cream cone.

"Ice cream!" He started for the door.

Sev grunted. Vin barely saw the fist coming for his face as he ran into it. Blackness flooded his vision.

## 5

Angela watched as Officer Harris lifted a piece of Gary's skin off the floor by the cell bars. The evidence of all she witnessed was right there in front of her, and she still couldn't believe it.

"It looks like some kind of silicon," Harris observed, dropping it back where he found it. "So let's review. You lost the ice cream bandit."

Angela grimaced. "I didn't lose him. People came and took him."

*People.*

*People came.*

*Freaking aliens came, melted off their skin, broke through bars without scratching them, and took my extraterrestrial prisoner with them.*

"Any idea who?" Harris prompted.

Angela shook her head in denial. "People."

"People," he repeated skeptically. "Fine. This is how we're going to spin it. Due to the high level of activity tonight in the casinos and on the strip, I ordered you to release Flame with a warning since our resources were stretched thin. He offered to pay for the ice cream, and we'll attribute the rest to a drunken stunt."

"I'm sorry, Harris. I know that I messed up." Angela wasn't sure what else she should say. She definitely couldn't tell the truth. She would lose her job faster than anything. And she needed this job. Her mother was depending on her getting a promotion.

"Yes. You did." Harris' expression showed little by way of sympathy.

Angela averted her eyes, unable to take the disappointment she saw in him. The truth was he should not have left her alone. Not on her first night as a trainee. His covering for her was as much for himself as it was for her.

"I'm going to let you off with a warning as well. This is your one slip up. Next time I won't be so lenient." Harris eyed the cell door with disgust before motioning to the silicone skin on the ground. "Get this cleaned up before you leave."

"What about Mags?"

"Does she know anything?"

Angela shook her head in denial. "I didn't say much. I just said that his brother came to pick him up."

"Good. We will leave it at that." Harris made a move to leave. He paused at the door. "I'm sorry, Angela. Based on tonight's performance I'm not sure you have what it takes to join our ranks. I'm hoping that you prove me wrong over the next several weeks."

"I will," she promised. "This will never happen again."

"It better not. The force isn't for everyone." Harris left.

Failure made her irritable and touchy. Her frustration at having botched her first night as a trainee was tinged with anger. Harris had thrown her into the deep end and left her alone to deal with it. Could she really blame him, though? She'd said she could handle it.

The measured control over her emotions left Angela the second she was alone. Her hands began to shake as she made her way across to the cell. She stared at the skin on the floor. Failure was only one of the many sensations crashing in on her and was soon replaced by fear.

Aliens. What did she do with the knowledge of aliens? She couldn't tell anyone, or they would think she was crazy. She needed this job. She needed not to be crazy. Aliens.

Vinglarkenbauer. Vin. Flame. Alien.

A significant part of her wanted to run away. Run out of the building. Run away from responsibility. Run from the city she had grown up in. But she couldn't leave her mother. And her mother couldn't come with her. Angela was trapped in Las Vegas.

She put on a pair of gloves. It took everything she had to reach down and quickly throw the skin into the garbage can. It squished between her fingers. She sprayed disinfectant on the floor and on the bars where the aliens had touched. She had no way of knowing if it would do any good.

When she finally clocked out and left the office, she was still trembling. She made her way warily down the hallway and into the teeming shopping center. She surveyed the crowd with a renewed appreciation and fear. How many aliens were out there? She would never have asked the question before tonight.

A group of young men passed by. One of them accidentally elbowed her.

Angela stiffened in alarm and lifted her arms in defense. "Watch where you're going." She couldn't help herself.

"Ooh, so scared of you, mall cop," a smart ass mocked, before two of his friends pulled him back into line.

"Asshole," Angela muttered under her breath as she spotted another group of men. A few of them were as tall as Vin, and she quickly sidestepped out of their path so they could pass. She made a beeline through the shopping complex's displays so she could study them. Their skin seemed normal enough, no weird stretching or melting. Three of them wore sunglasses, but the rest of their eyes weren't metallic.

Vin had looked human. She'd assumed he was human. Why wouldn't she think that? And she'd been wrong. She saw how his metallic eyes changed and he melted the metal handcuffs holding him together. He could've escaped at any time. Instead, he sat in the cell talking to her as if he was a human talking to another human. That is until he said he was an alien.

*I'm going crazy. I'm going crazy. Tonight did not happen. I'm overworked, and I'm stressed. I did not see alien hands. I did not see Vin melt off his handcuffs.*

It was hard to tell if this was a case of extreme craziness. And if Vin was highly intelligent, then she couldn't be blamed for doubting herself. Hell, mental asylums were full of his kind.

Angela looked at everyone she passed but did not meet their eyes. It was the usual Vegas crowd—drunk tourists, a few parents with their children, brides-maids, groomsmen, a family wearing the same bright orange reunion T-shirts as they made their way from shop to shop. Several of them played some kind of scavenger hunt game on their phones, which was very popular this year. Everything looked normal.

Angela tried to appear as if nothing was wrong as she made her way out of the building. The walk to the car felt like it took a very long time. She just wanted to get home. She wanted to see her mother. She wanted out of Vegas.

The entire journey home one word kept cycling her brain over and over. *Aliens. Aliens. Aliens.*

## 6

VIN STARED up at the ceiling as he lay tied to the bed. His brother had left him to suffer without his precious ice cream. Though the more time that past and the less sugar that remained in his system, he began to realize he might be slightly obsessed with the delicious creamy treat. The headache was the worst part. Then the shaking. And then the deep cravings. He wanted that taste in his mouth, to feel his internal temperature drop to euphoria, and the rush of his blood as the sugar absorbed into his system.

However, as the headache eased, and the shaking became a tiny tremor, another obsession filled his mind. How could he think of ice cream when there was Angela?

Angela and ice cream.

Vin closed his eyes and smiled.

"Stop that," Sev ordered. "You're looking obsessively disturbed again."

Vin opened one eye to look at the doorway. "Untie me."

"Not a chance," Sev answered. "You're on lockdown. Gary said they are bringing you an injection and it could take a couple of days to process through your system."

"You hit me." Vin looked more fully at his brother, seeing red marks on his face and neck. "But it looks like someone hit you back." He stiffened and pulled against his restraints, trying to break free.

"Don't bother. Those are crafted out of alien metal. You're not heating your way out of them."

"What did you do to Angela? Is she unharmed? What happened after you struck me? Who hit you?" Vin's heart beat erratically. When Galaxy Alien Mail Order Brides uploaded information into their brains about Earth culture, one of the warnings was how delicate Earthlings were. The implication had been that the women bruised easily, and rough sex had been warned against, but the same would hold true for brawling. One hit from Sev could've snapped her spine.

"I did nothing to your zookeeper. She is fine. We left her unharmed. You had caused enough trouble, and I didn't want to bring any more of the authorities down on our heads." Sev grimaced. "Unfortunately your cousin did not get the memo."

"What is the memo?"

"Some kind of Earth document. Like a mini news chip they pass around. I heard a local say it," Sev explained.

"And Kal didn't get it?" Vin was confused. "Where is Kal?"

Sev tried to look stern, but a telltale excitement lit up his eyes. There had been a fight.

"What did I miss? What did you two do?"

"Oh, my brother, you missed the fun. While you were busy cramming your face full of alien food and hanging out in a prison cell, we took on an entire casino of assailants and an Earth savant. Kal fell in love. She was kidnapped. And we rescued her. People were running. Fists were flying. Guns were shooting. Kal sent several of the men flying." Sev threw several pretend punches to narrate his actions. "We narrowly escaped with our lives, but in the end, we saved the girl. We're heroes."

"You're making up stories," Vin said skeptically. "Kal fell in love?"

The rest was believable.

Sev's expression sobered. "He thinks he is going to stay here on Earth with her. There's no way I'm letting that happen. Kal may be a screw up, but he is our screw up. We will not leave this planet unless all of us are on the transport back home."

"Kal found love?" Vin thought of Angela and wondered what it would feel like to have a woman's love. He'd had a woman's body many times, but her love?

"Yes. Kal found love. Is there something wrong with your brain?" Sev frowned. "It is that woman from the restaurant he spent the last week searching for. He seems to think that Galaxy Brides can't make us return if we don't want to. I don't care what Galaxy Alien Mail Order Brides has to say. He is coming back with us. He is our family, and he is coming home."

Vin wasn't as firm in his stance as Sev was. Yes, he liked the comfort of the underground settlement, the familiarity of the rock walls and knowing his neighbors. There was comfort in the idea that when something happened, the settlement would come to his aid. He was not so sure Earth humans would help their neighbors if they were in trouble. The truth was he didn't know Earth humans well at all. Most of what he knew was what he had seen on the rogue transmission waves floating around space.

At the same time, though, he could see the appeal of a planet like Earth with its fresh air and sunlight that didn't blister off the skin. Living and working underground in the mines was a hard existence. It wasn't one he shied away from as a Killian. He came from generations of ashers, but he also didn't wish to die young. His plan was to find another way to live within Frxsolis.

"Are you listening to me?" Sev demanded.

Vin nodded even though he hadn't been. "Sure. Kal comes with us, or you'll start an intergalactic event the Federation can't ignore."

Sev arched an eyebrow. "I said that I told Galaxy Brides I wanted them to bring us a transport and shuttle us off this damn planet. We should never have come here—not to a place that doesn't know aliens exist. It is a failed experiment conducted by a substandard corporation with little experience. You saw the two clowns they sent with me to rescue you. Gary and Bob? Are you kidding me? Yes, they have skills, but the size of their heads hardly attributes to blending in. They claim they want to stay hidden, and yet Gary melted his skin suit off."

"What did they say about the girl following you around?" Vin asked with a smirk.

Sev frowned. "That joke has lost any hope of being funny. You and Kal both need to stop telling it. There is no woman following me around, and I refuse to let you cast me into paranoia over it."

"I'm feeling better," Vin said. "Can you untie me now?"

"No," Sev dismissed. "I can't risk you running off, so get comfortable. Between the fight in the casino, the assailants coming after Kal and his woman, and your arrest because you overindulged in ice cream of all things, we are on lockdown. Next move is the transport taking us out of Vegas."

"If we are on lockdown where is Kal?"

"He's in the other room with the woman he..." Sev tilted his head and listened. "Blasted space holes, where the eternal furnace did they go? I'll be back. At least I know you're not going anywhere."

Vin watched his brother storm out of the room to look for their cousin. He grinned and thought of the Earth slang he'd heard a couple of young men say before jumping into the giant pond by the dancing fountain, *Challenge accepted.*

Now, to find a way out of the impossible chains that bound his wrists together. Vin lifted is arms and began to use the chain to saw back and forth behind his head. The alien metal might not melt, but that didn't mean the Vegas bed wouldn't come apart.

Whether it was Bravon, or Earth, or any two-bit fuel dock floating around space, one thing remained true when it came to women. They wanted their man to prove their worth to them. And it wasn't achieved through some calculated method manipulating the laws of attraction, despite the dating advice Galaxy Brides had given them.

"Greetings, Vin," Gary said from the door.

Vin stopped sawing his arms.

The Galaxy Brides employee's hand suit had been repaired, and he again looked like a deformed Earth human. "I brought the injection. This should remove the excess sugar from your system and flush out the Earth toxins. As long as you do not eat—"

"I don't want it," Vin dismissed. "I feel fine."

"Your brother insists that we administer it to you," Gary stated. He didn't need to spell it out. The man was more afraid of Sev than of Vin. "This will help you rest."

"I don't want to rest."

When Gary drew the injector close to his thigh, Vin jerked his leg away.

"Listen, Gary, I can't sleep now. You know that

woman? Angela? I really like her. I want to find her. How about you free me so that I may do so? Isn't that why we are all here? To find women?"

"I will make a notation in your file about Angela." Gary again leaned over with the injector. Vin tried to kick him away, but the little being was surprisingly strong. He gripped Vin's thigh and injected him in the butt with the medicine. "You will rest now."

Vin's vision blurred. This wasn't over. If Kal had found love, then Vin could find love.

Angela was worth it. He would prove his worth to her by escaping and going to her. She might very well be the one.

It was by sheer power and force of will that one proved their love for a woman. What better way to begin his pursuit by breaking out of the shackles he was bound by?

His vision continued to blur as he endeavored to stay awake. He had to find Angela. Just as soon as he finished this nap.

## 7

"MAGS?" Vin questioned, pausing on the busy side-walk as he waited for the response. He was still a little wobbly from the injection, but that didn't matter. Once he'd regained consciousness, escape had been easy. He doubted the hotel would think too kindly about the destroyed bed, but he couldn't worry about things like that. He needed to find Angela.

"What?" a surly male voice demanded.

"I need Mags," Vin insisted into the phone. "Mags answers the phone. Angela lets it ring, so I need Mags so she can get Angela."

"I don't know no Mags. This is an emergency line, sir, take your dating life else—"

Vin hung up before dialing the next number on

the directory listing for casino security. Heavy chains hung around his neck like a scarf while binding to the cuffs on his wrists. He wore clean clothes— thanks to his brother bothering to change his shirt before he chained him up—and had wiped all traces of dried ice cream off his face. He wanted to look respectable when he found Angela.

No one answered after twenty rings, so he directed the cellular phone to the next number on the list. Portable communication devices were handy. He didn't care for the radiation waves he saw coming off them, but they were useful.

"You have reached Ma Clary's Investigations," a pleasant woman said.

"I need to speak with Mags," Vin stated.

The woman ignored him and kept talking. "We are not in the office right now."

"I don't care where you are right now. I am not in an office," he said over the voice that kept talking. "I need to find Mags."

"You know what to do at the beep," she continued.

"I do not know what to do at the beep," Vin insisted. "What is the beep?"

A beep sounded. Vin looked at the phone and

then around the immediate area. What was he supposed to do?

"Hey, look, it's the ice cream man!" a teenager yelled, pointing at him. The kid wore a backward cap over his shaggy blond hair.

"Are you what is at the beep?" Vin asked.

"Yeah, I got the beat, ice cream man. You got the beat, ice cream man?" the kid inquired, doing a little dance on the sidewalk. The others with him laughed and clapped their hands.

Vin frowned and glanced around the sidewalk before turning his attention back to the kid. "I do not have a beet. They are indigestible vegetables. I prefer ice cream."

The teens laughed harder.

"Where you off to, ice cream man?" The girl who spoke gave a small strut as she stood next to the dancing kid. Her short skirt was held up with a giant belt that engulfed her waist. "Want to come hang with us?"

"I do hang up," he stated. "I cannot connect to Mags' phone."

"Cool, cool," dancing boy said, grinning widely. "Hey, can I take a selfie with you?"

"I do not know what you are saying, or why you are talking to me. This beep is over," Vin dismissed.

Before striding away, he advised, "And you should pull your pants up or else you will trip."

"Fuck you, too, man. No need to be an ass," the teen yelled. "Your video wasn't that funny, anyway."

Vin didn't have time to beep with the strange locals. Las Vegas was a big territory, and he needed to find Angela. He again lifted the phone and dialed. Mags had to answer sometime.

"Damn," Vin shouted up at the man through the open passenger door of the tall vehicle.

Vin hoped this guy liked him enough to give him a ride. The last carload had told him they didn't give rides to crazy guys, and that he needed to learn to chill out and be cool. The smoke coming from their car smelled funny, and he did not trust the pilot of that vehicle with his bloodshot eyes and giggling nature.

The truck before the smokestack wanted to trade favors, but apparently had no need for Vin's skills as an ash miner. The man also apparently had eaten too much because he'd unbuttoned his pants while he talked. Before the glutton, there had been a long, black car where one of the girls had thrown something akin to tiny boxer shorts at his head. He dodged them and then threw the clothing back at her, smacking her in the face. She was not pleased. Apparently, Vin did not understand the game and was not let into the vehicle.

"Hoover Dam?" The guy called out from inside the hauling vehicle that had pulled over to the side of the road.

"Damn!" Vin answered to show he was cool, and not crazy. He liked the sound of the word. Locals seemed to use it often as an exclamation of joy or approval. Men said it when they saw an attractive woman or when they came close to winning at the tables. Since he wanted to find Angela, who was *damn!* he thought it an appropriate time to use it to express his mission.

If he managed to win the favor with the pilot of the large hauling vehicle, then the man could drop him off at a place called Sunny Side. That is where Mags said Angela was.

"Well, you're in luck. This fertilizer is destined for the same area. If you don't mind the smell, hop on in," the man invited. "I wouldn't mind the company. Been a long haul."

Vin glanced at the back toward the cargo. The metabolic composition of the load was comparable with what was in the soil on the wheels of the vehicle. The smell was a small inconvenience if this man would take him to Angela. He gave a small hop and then climbed into the truck.

"They call me Skeeter."

"They call me Flame."

Skeeter glanced over Vin's shackles. "Is that what you young generation call Cos-Play?"

"Cos-Play," Vin muttered to himself. He liked the sound of the game and so he nodded. He briefly wondered if Angela would play it with him.

"Don't get it myself." The man put the car into gear and began to drive. "Where are you coming from?"

"Canada," Vin said.

"Where are you headed?"

"I'm going to find Angela."

"Ah, a girl," the man chuckled. "Ain't it always about a girl."

"I cannot answer that. All I know is I need to find Angela."

"Well, I can drop you off at Boulder City." Skeeter navigated his vehicle into thicker traffic. "That do?"

"I'm not sure. Is that where Sunny Side is located?"

"I'm not sure what Sunny Side is."

"Mags said it is a place with lots of crazy, old, ill people." Vin sighed, saddened at how Earth sometimes appeared to be a highly segregated planet based on wealth, health, and beauty. "But Mags is a little difficult to comprehend."

"Old, huh?" The man pressed a device on his dashboard, touching several Earth symbols before saying, "Found it. Sunny Side. It's a nursing facility just five miles from here. It's not on the way to Boulder City, at least, not really, but for love, I can drop you close to where you need to be."

"Thank you." Vin smiled.

"Your girl a nurse there?"

"I am not sure. That is where Mags told me she would be tonight."

The rest of the short journey was quiet. It gave Vin time to study the atmosphere surrounding Sunny Side. He watched tiny streaks come off the lights, and from the overhead electrical wires.

Skeeter pulled off the busy roadway and eased them along a side street. He gestured out the window. "The building you're looking for is just down there. I'd take you closer, but it's a maze of one-way streets, and I need to get back on the interstate."

Visions of Angela came flooding back as Vin opened the door and slowly stepped out.

"Good luck to you, boy," Skeeter called.

The door of the truck slammed shut behind him. Vin gave a small jump of surprise and turned to see the vehicle pull away from the curb. Skeeter revved the engine a few times and lifted his hand. Vin returned the gesture as he was left alone on the dark, abandoned street.

## 8

"Mom?" Angela stepped quietly into her mother's private room. She'd decorated it as close to her childhood home as she could, but there was no hiding the medical equipment on the walls or the fact the living space consisted of one room and a bathroom. Some days she wondered if her mother even saw the rose painting or the floral curtains. "Are you awake? It's me, Angela."

What had started as simple forgetfulness had deteriorated into severe dementia. Her mother's memory had worsened from forgetting where she parked the car to forgetting her own name, the time they lived in, and the fact she even had a daughter. The doctors had said many things, using many keywords—early onset, rapid decline, reduced ability

MICHELLE M. PILLOW

to perform everyday tasks, doing everything we can. Their statements held no comfort for a daughter alone in the world.

Her mother had always been a night owl, so it was no surprise that she was still awake in her chair. She held her purse on her lap, rocking back and forth as if riding in a car. Angela wished she could crawl inside the woman's mind and see what she was seeing.

"Hi, Mom," Angela said. She set her empty coffee cup on an end table. It would have probably been in her best interest to go home and sleep, but instead, she chose to load up on extra shots of espresso and drive to see her mom. Sometimes, a girl just needed her mother. "How are you tonight?"

The woman smiled and nodded as she would any stranger on a small town street. Angela took a seat on the twin size bed to be closer to her.

"I had to see you. I missed you," Angela tried to sound positive and conversational. Her mother nodded and didn't make eye contact. This apparently was one of the days she wasn't speaking too much. "It was another rough day at work. Harris doesn't trust me to do anything. He rechecks all my paperwork. He wouldn't even let me talk to any of the people we stopped. It's frustrating, and the

74

worst part is I know he has every right to doubt my skills."

Her mother didn't answer.

"I tried really hard, just like you would have told me to do, and I was doing great. I made that supervised arrest I told you about the other night. I got this man to come with us without force or incident. It was mainly a disorderly conduct call. You know how crazy the strip is, but I handled it."

Her mother nodded several times. Angela pretended like the woman actually listened. The truth was she had no way of knowing what her mother heard.

"Then everything went wrong. I was left alone to babysit the man in a holding cell, and I lost him." Angela gave a small, humorless laugh. She'd told this story to her mother before, but she had no one else to talk to as she rehashed the incident. "I lost a man who was locked up in a cage. Can you believe that? It's not like I was watching a criminal mastermind either. Just some dude who happened to like ice cream a little too much. I freaking lost the ice cream bandit. Some security guard cop trainee I turned out to be. I'll probably be the reason they stop the pilot program."

Her mother blinked and briefly looked in her

direction. Recognition did not dawn on her frail features.

"I thought I could just keep my head down and put it behind me, but apparently, a bunch of kids with cell phones recorded the incident and posted it all over the Internet. It's gone viral. The higher-ups are beginning to ask questions. I mean, Harris said in our report that we let the man go with a warning due to the high number of incidences that night, but I feel his irritation every time the subject comes up. He looks at me, and I just know he's thinking of ways to get me fired."

"I wonder what time it is," her mother whispered, as if to herself.

"It's after ten, Mom," Angela answered.

Her mother nodded. "Hmm, it's late again."

"I promise I'm trying, Mom." Angela looked around the small room. Her mother had worked so hard her entire life. She deserved more than painted brick walls and a tiny window disguised by oversized curtains. At least Sunny Side was clean. The other facility she could afford had been questionable at best. "I think I have a buyer for that painting grandpa left us. We never really liked it, anyway. Remember how you always said the woman's face looked like she was half cow? Apparently, she was. I found out it was supposed to be a modern representation of some Egyptian lesser goddess. The money from the sale should be good for a couple of months at the new place. After that, I'll figure something out. We need to move fast while they have an opening at Memory Meadows. I think you'll love it there. There will be more space, and I'll be able to bring some of your stuff out of storage."

"Are you hungry, dear?" her mother asked, the gentle voice both familiar and distant. "You look awfully thin. How long since you ate something? There is a soup kitchen just two blocks East. I volunteer there sometimes. Tell them Connie sent you. They'll make sure you have a safe place to rest and a warm meal. You look like you need a rest."

"Thank you, Connie, I'll do that," Angela answered.

Her mother nodded and smiled, happy with the response. "That's good."

"I saw an alien." Angela wondered how it would sound saying the sentence out loud for the first time as if verbalizing it would make it either true or false. "Several aliens. And not illegal ones coming over the border for work but real aliens from outer space. He was really handsome. I mean, daydream handsome. I can't stop thinking about him. That has to be some kind of alien chemical drugging effect, right? I just want to see him again to prove he's real. Not that I would date someone who I had to help arrest, or an alien, or an escapee, but he was something. I don't feel crazy, but I couldn't have seen that, right? I mean, if I can't function who is going to take care of things? And if I'm not crazy that means there are aliens in Las Vegas. I could use your advice, Mom. I'm not doing so well."

Angela tried to take her mother's hand, but the woman gave her a strange look and pulled her purse closer to her stomach.

"How about we read a little?" Angela opened the nightstand to take out a book and settled back on the bed. "Your favorite. Pride and Prejudice."

"I cannot hear her speak. How do you know what she answers?"

Angela gasped, sitting up on the bed as she dropped the book to her side. "Vin?"

Vin stepped into the room. Angela instantly went to stand in front of her mother, blocking her from the alien's view.

"What are you doing here?" Angela demanded. How much did he hear? "You can't be in here. This is a private facility. How did you find me?"

"Mags," Vin answered. "And Skeeter."

"Mags and Skeeter? I don't understand. Who is Skeeter?"

"Skeeter gave me a ride with his fertilizer load. I told him about you, and he found this place for me so I could see you. Before that, I called security offices listed in Las Vegas and explained that I needed to talk to Mags because she answers the phone. You let the phone ring, so I needed her to get you for me. When I was finally able to speak to her, Mags told me where to find you. She said you always come here after a hard day. Was today a hard day?" He smiled, as if he expected her to think being stalked by an alien was normal.

"Mags should not be giving out my information. It is not appropriate for you to be here." Angela had a few choice words she'd like to say to the receptionist. "You need to leave."

"Why was it a hard day?" he asked.

Angela's eyes opened wide as she stared at him. "Are you kidding me?"

"I do not believe so. I'm trying to talk to you so you'll date me. I can't stop thinking about you." The words were guileless in their delivery. He looked at her with the same, open expression he'd had while walking toward the holding cell.

"It was hard because aliens came to my work this

week and freed the man I was supposed to be guarding. Try explaining how a cell door is unlocked without force, the security cameras didn't record any footage, a prisoner escapes a holding cell, and I don't have a scratch on me. I looked like an idiot to my supervisor. He probably thinks I just let you go. Each time I try to get past it something else happens. Today I learned that we've evidently gone viral. I tanked any chance I had at a promotion to a new liaison officer position, and, oh yeah, thanks to that my mother is probably going to remain in this overcrowded place without access to the therapy treatments she desperately needs. It's all I can do to afford her a private room here. The only saving grace is that the staff is kind, but even they are overworked."

Angela breathed heavily. She realized that in her tirade she had stepped over to where he stood and now glared up at him. Intense heat radiated off his body, seeming to soak into her skin.

"Jim!" her mother cried out in excitement.

Angela felt the woman move behind her and quickly pulled away from Vin to stop her from approaching.

"It's me, Connie. How have you been? I was so sorry to hear about you and Sheila." Her mother's hands shook slightly as she held them out.

Vin arched a brow in confusion. Damn, if he didn't look human.

"Mom, stop," Angela tried to pull her mother back.

"I left money on the table for the bill, miss," her mother answered, shooing her away.

"Mom, it's me, Angela."

"I left you a tip, even though the sandwich was cold in the middle. I know that was the kitchen's doing, not you, dear," her mother insisted, "but you should say something to your bosses and let them know it's not your fault. A woman has to stand up for herself in the workplace."

Angela felt tears burn her eyes, but nodded. "Thank you, ma'am. I will."

Vin gently took her mother's hands in his. "My name is Vin, not Jim."

"Oh, excuse me," her mother laughed. "I must have left my glasses at home. Of course, you're not Jim." She looked up at the man's face. "But you are a handsome one, aren't you?"

"Oh, gawd, Mom, don't," Angela said, hoping to stop her mother from flirting with the alien. It was bad enough Angela was attracted to him.

"Thank you, Connie," he stated. "I think you are beautiful as well."

"Not helping," Angela said to Vin. He ignored her.

"Are you single?" her mother asked.

"I am trying not to be." Vin lifted his eyes to Angela and winked. She shook her head in denial, wanting him to stop encouraging her mother down this strange path.

"Do you work?" her mother continued as if Angela was not there.

"Yes. I work in the ash mines, but I hope to open a business of some sort very soon. There is nowhere to go in the mines but deeper into the ground."

"Hard work is good, but so is ambition. Do you dance?"

"Yes. I have been practicing the local dances. Would you like to see?"

Her mother nodded. Vin didn't let go of the woman's hands as he circled his hips and upper body in something akin to a male stripper on a stage.

Angela made a weak noise of protest. She had to stop this.

"Good," her mother stated with a nod of approval. "A man should know how to dance. Do you own a suit?"

"This isn't happening," Angela mumbled.

"I own jeans and t-shirts. I am a working man, and that is what working men wear here."

"Hmm, a man should always own at least one suit. But, that's easy enough to rectify. You should buy yourself a nice suit." Her mother's voice dipped meaningfully as she added, "Women appreciate a nice suit."

Angela grimaced. Was she really watching her mother flirt? She lifted up her hands to try to break into the conversation. She stepped closer to their joined hands. "Ok, let's stop before she invites you to the High School sock hop. This is just weird."

Vin gave her a stern look. The expression took her by surprise, and she stopped short of placing her hands on theirs to pull them apart. He turned his attention back to her mother.

"You have kind eyes. I've got a sense about these things. You should meet my daughter," her mother offered. "I think you'd like her. She works too much trying to take care of me, even though I tell her I'm fine. She thinks I don't know, but she has been going into the bank and paying my mortgage herself instead of taking the check I give her to the post office. She sneaks groceries into my cabinets, too. She's a good girl but works too much. I'd like to see her have some fun before she's my age."

"If she is like you at your age, I think she would be wonderful to meet," Vin said. It was a strangely worded compliment, but then what was normal about this situation?

"Not that it matters, but she is very beautiful. Here," her mother lifted her hands and stepped back as if excited, "I have her picture in my purse. It's an older picture, but you'll see for yourself." Her mother moved back toward her chair and picked up her purse. Setting it on her lap, she fumbled with the latch for a second before beginning to rock back and forth as she had been doing when Angela first walked in.

"Thank you for being nice to her," Angela said. "I haven't seen her that talkative in a long time."

Vin nodded. "How long has she had the brain deterioration?"

"A few years. It's become worse in the last six months. New therapies are being offered at Memory Meadows, but they're expensive and, since they are experimental, the insurance company doesn't want to cover it. They already act like they're waiting for the perfect excuse to dump her as a customer."

Angela looked at her mother. "I wish I knew what was going on in her brain. Is she happy? Is she scared? What does she need?"

"She is a mother," Vin stated as if it were the easiest question in the world. "She needs for her daughter to be happy and safe. She said as much just now. She worries about you. You work too hard, and she'd like you to have fun."

"She doesn't know what she is saying," Angela denied.

"You have to listen differently," Vin said. He turned his attention to the older woman. "Connie?"

"Yes?"

"What are you waiting for?" he asked.

"The bus, silly. This is a bus stop. It's been a long day, and I'm tired. I just want to go to bed," she said.

"How...?" Angela looked at Vin in amazement. "How do you do that? I can't get her to answer me."

"I'm a new voice," he surmised. "Perhaps I do not stir her memories like you do."

It was true. She doubted her mother had ever heard an accent quite like Vin's before.

"Come on, Mom, ah, Connie. Time to sleep." Angela pulled the covers down on the bed. It was a small feat, but Angela felt like it was a giant win. Her mother was waiting at the bus station so she could go home to bed. To Vin, she said, "Could you wait outside? I'm going to help her change her clothes."

Vin nodded and left. Angela stared after him for

a long moment. Suddenly, the fact he was an alien didn't matter. In a few minutes, he'd made more progress with her mother than any of the doctors for the last six months.

"I always liked that boy," her mother said.

"Me, too," Angela answered. "I think I like him too."

## 9

"W<small>HAT'S WITH THE CHAINS</small>?" Angela's soft voice drifted in from somewhere behind him. Vin had waited for her on the front step of the old building as she tended to her mother. "Don't tell me you were arrested a second time."

"I will not tell you that." He lifted his wrists to look at the heavy shackles. "My brother tried to keep me from running off, so he had the Galaxy Alien Mail Order Bride people chain me to the bed and inject me with something to get the ice cream out of my system."

"Why don't you melt them off?"

"Alien metal." He shook his wrists to make the chains clink before dropping his hands. "I tried, but they're stuck."

"Let me see. Maybe I can pick the lock or at least pry it open." Angela stepped before him and took his hands in hers. She examined his wrists. The darker light was pierced by the glow from a streetlamp. It illuminated the top of her head. In the distance, the sound of traffic reminded him of how much life this planet carried on its back. "There isn't a lock, not even a seam. How did they put them on you—"

When she lifted her face, Vin kissed her. Her lips were parted in speech, and he took advantage of the opening. His tongue brushed along her mouth, dipping inside. To his surprise, she didn't back away. When he finally pulled back, she was holding onto the front of his shirt and breathing hard.

"You're very warm," she whispered. "Is it normal for you to be this warm?"

"This planet is very cool," he said. "Normally, I am warmer."

"How are you here?" She didn't let go of him. "Why? How long have your people been here? Does the government know? Are you in trouble? Are you safe? Are you...?"

"I understand you have questions." Vin would rather have kept kissing her. "I came to Earth by spaceship. My cousin signed us up for a service to meet women who may become our wives. None of us wish to mate with the women on our planet. We are not technically related to everyone, but it is a very small gene pool and...do you understand?"

"Of course. Over time, intermarriage within a village could cause harm. I remember reading something about that in my anthropology class before I dropped out of college and got a job." She pulled away from him. "So you're just here to marry anyone who will have you?"

"I am here for the free vacation that signing up allowed us to take." He grinned. "I did not expect to meet anyone like you. I thought the Galaxy Brides Corporation was a joke, but perhaps they know something I don't. They might even employ psychics."

"So, you just arrived here?"

"Me, yes. Others have been visiting Earth since the beginning of your time, from what I understand. Officially, your people as a whole do not know aliens are real, and no first contact has been made. However, the public being unaware is not the same as the secret governmental groups being uninformed of life in other universes. Someone sold you the technology to create cellular phones and computers. I only wish they would have given you the more modern version, not the primitive stuff you all carry around."

"What you're saying is terrifying, but logically I know today is no different than yesterday in the fact that life is what it is and we'll continue to go on." She glanced up at the building to where her mother's room was. "And none of that changes the fact I need to find a second job to pay for Memory Meadows."

"Would it help if I let you arrest me again? Would that make this an easy day instead of a hard one?" He held out his hands, willing to let her take him back to the cage. "Would that get you the promotion?"

"No. At this point, I think that would just make things worse. You'd have to explain how you escaped. There would be more charges. Or my supervisor might become angry over the fact I took matters into my own hands and arrested you without his permission or authority. No charges are pending for you, so you're free to go."

"Are you free to go with me?" He smiled and tried gallantly to hold out his arm as he'd seen on the transmission waves.

She understood his gesture and slipped her hand onto his arm. "Are you asking me to go to your suite again?"

"If that is your wish, but I thought your mother told me I needed to take you out to have fun." He began to walk the way he'd come, down the dark street.

She pulled his arm to stop him. "I take it this Skeeter guy isn't waiting for you, is he?"

"No, he left."

"I'm assuming you don't have a car. How about I drive us?"

"Yes." Vin smiled. "That will be much faster than asking people for rides. And I know the perfect place to take you for fun."

Angela smiled. The glint in her eye was a memory he would cherish forever, regardless of which planet he ended up on.

He hadn't known her for long, but everything about her was right. Right for him. The fact her mother was the center of her universe proved what type of the person she was—family oriented, kind hearted, sweet. And then there were her looks.

"Damn," Vin sighed.

"What?" Angela looked into his eyes.

"Nothing." Vin wanted to kiss her again, but he couldn't stop admiring her. He raised his hands to touch her face but stopped when the shackles clanked. He found them mildly annoying. "Come. I know a place that will be fun."

"I am hungry," Angela confessed.

"Good." Vin motioned at her to follow him as he walked away.

"Uh, my car is this way," she called after him.

"Oh." Vin stopped and started walking back-ward. Angela laughed.

ANGELA PULLED the car into the all-night diner parking lot and glanced up at the giant ice cream cone blinking on the neon sign. "I wonder what made you pick this place."

"There is something appealing about it, and it looks fun." Vin grinned as he reached to open his door.

"I'm not taking you in there," Angela stated. The drive had been surprisingly pleasant, and the conversation between them flowed as if they had known each other for years. Some of his assumptions about Earth culture were hilarious, but it was easy to see he had a positive outlook and enjoyed life. Maybe his attitude was because he'd worked so hard in the mining business, which sounded about as safe as being trapped in the Monongah, West Virginia coal mines at the turn of the twentieth century. Hard manual labor could often equal hard play.

He shut the door and stayed in the car. "But, what about the fun?"

She again looked at the neon sign. The reminder made her feel like she was harboring a fugitive. Fine, the escaped ice cream bandit was hardly on America's Most Wanted list, but still. "I don't think ice cream is the best idea for you. I saw what happened last time. I *arrested* you last time."

His smile fell some. "But I enjoy ice cream. The sugar makes me tingle."

"I'm sure it does," she laughed. "You kind of remind me of a little kid who's given it for the first time, eats too much of it, and then runs around on a sugar high like a screaming maniac before crashing."

"I don't like the crashing, so I eat more."

"Exactly my point." She frowned. "Wait, have you eaten anything else since you've been here?"

Vin shook his head in denial. "Sev said the food here was too colorful, so the waitress suggested we have a milkshake that was white. I did. Sev did not. Then I had another. Then another. Then the boy at the counter told me I could have a chocolate one. The girl said I should try the special. It was a beet kale health shake smoothie and tasted awful. I found out it didn't have ice cream in it. So, then I had a strawberry ice cream shake before trying a soft serve ice cream cone. Then—"

"I'm getting the picture," Angela interrupted. "Listen, ice cream is well and good in moderation. But how about we get you something else to try? Maybe a nice, healthy salad?"

"I don't think I like healthy. That beet kale was not nice."

"All right, then a burger and fries?"

"My cousin likes triple burgers," Vin said. "All right. I will try that. Kal and I like many of the same things."

"Not healthy, but not sugar, so we'll call this a win," Angela mumbled to herself, wondering if she was the right person to ambassador an alien around town. Looking at him, it was easy to forget he wasn't from Earth. She had to keep reminding herself of that fact. "Listen, before we go in, I wanted to make sure I thanked you for being nice to my mom. Some people get uncomfortable around the sick. She doesn't smile a whole lot anymore, and you made her smile. That means something to me."

"Why wouldn't I be nice to her? Connie is a nice

lady," Vin said. "Plus, she thinks you should be with me."

Angela laughed. "I hardly think knowing each other for such a short period of time can equal marriage. It normally takes years to get to that step."

"Why?" Vin looked confused. "If I know my mind, and you know your mind, then what is the issue? I know plenty of happy Killian couples that knew each other mere hours before marrying."

"I don't think Earthlings work like that."

"Killians do, and you are humanoid like me." He turned to face her, lifting his leg up slightly onto the front seat. "Close your eyes and listen to your feelings. Sense them radiating out of you and then follow where they lead. Love and marriage and life are not complicated things to figure out once you accept that nothing is perfect. It starts with feelings and then ends with a decision."

Angela hesitated, not sure she wanted to try his experiment. "I understand your point, but how do you know you're not going to marry someone who beats you or cheats on you? Or has some secret foot bondage fetish? Some things only time can tell, and so time must be taken."

"Why would a person beat or cheat?" Vin frowned. "I know of this concept, but I don't understand it. Why decide to marry and allow yourself to love if you plan on betraying that? Love is the simplest of things, and the most beautiful. I think you are complicating it too much." He reached to touch her inner thigh. Her breathing deepened, and she stiffened at the acute awareness she felt at his touch. The heat from his finger seemed to sear into her skin, not hurting but definitely noticeable. Responsiveness coursed through her, heating her blood with the promise of sexual release. "You let your thoughts swim around too much in here."

Angela glanced down at her thighs.

"This is where the Earth humanoid brain is, right?"

Angela couldn't help the small laugh. She took his hand in his and drew his fingers to her forehead. "Close, but my brain is here."

"Strange. A woman on the street told me men think with their penis heads, so I just assumed the human brain was between the legs." Vin sighed. "Though, that is good. It appears our biology is closer than I thought." He touched his chest. "But I was trying to make a point. When I look down, I see my energy reaching toward you like tiny fingers floating in the air. I feel it coming out of me, and I feel it being returned by you. It is lust, yes, but it is stronger than that. I'm looking at it right now. The Reticulan medical missionaries said that I have a genetic anomaly for our kind that allows me to visually detect radiation and energy more vividly than others. Our energies blend well."

As he said the words, Angela felt the energy he spoke of. It grew stronger the more she allowed herself to pay attention to it. She'd felt it the moment she'd touched him beside the ice cream vendor. His chin and lips had been covered with the sticky, melting treat. She'd been trying to make a good impression on Harris, so she hadn't given the feelings much credence.

"Close your eyes," he whispered.

This time, she did as he requested. She took a deep breath, and then another, letting herself feel without thinking. Her nerve endings tingled. His naturally warm body drew her toward him. She imagined tiny threads pulling them closer together.

His mouth brushed against hers in a gentle kiss. Her lips parted, and she traced the seam of his mouth with her tongue. Soon the kiss was deepened, and her hands became mindless wanderers, groping him like a person starved for affection.

It became impossible to tell where her feelings began and his ended. Flame was the perfect name for him because that was what he was, a flame drawing her in, burning passion into her veins with each touch. He was light and warmth, and everything she needed in that primitive moment to survive.

He suddenly stopped kissing her and pulled back. "Someone is watching us."

It took Angela a moment to focus on what he said. The sound of their heavy breathing filled the car, and she turned to look out the windows. "Where?"

"I am not sure, but close." Vin frowned, studying the parking lot. He motioned toward a darkened corner. "There, I believe."

"So what if some perv is in their car watching us kiss?" Angela dismissed.

"We should leave," Vin stated, appearing concerned as he looked out of the window toward the shadow.

"Is someone after you?" she asked.

"My brother will not be happy I left the hotel room to find you. I am not sure Galaxy Brides Corporation will care unless Sev threatens them again. He wants to leave. My cousin and I want to stay."

Angela wanted him to stay. The idea of him leaving, when she was just getting to know him, caused a strange sense of fear and loss inside of her. If Galaxy

Brides was looking for him, she was going to make sure they didn't find him. She started the car. "Well, I'm hungry. If we're not going inside, I'll take us to a fast food drive thru. Then we'll go back to my house. No one will look for you there."

There was a naivety about him that Angela liked, an innocence that drew her to him. His connecting with her mother was like icing on the cake. In the past, a couple of would-be boyfriends had come close to winning her heart. The stumbling block for both eligible men had been her need to take care of her mother.

Her wellbeing was paramount to Angela. There were only the two of them, her and mom.

"Well?" Vin smiled. "Are we going to go?"

"Yes, of course." Angela's smile felt genuine for once. It wasn't forced or fake. It came from somewhere deep within, and the reason for it was the strange person sitting in her passenger seat.

"Good. I want to drive through the food. That sounds like fun." Vin's eyes were wide with anticipation. "We can get completely covered in it!"

"IT'S NOT FANCY," Angela stated as she opened the apartment door, "but it's close to Sunny Side and work so I can't complain."

Vin stood in a hallway of evenly spaced doors, each distinguished only by a number painted on the dark wall next to them. His expression was unusually solemn as he stared at a nearby door.

"Is everything all right?" She touched his arm. "I know it's not like how you described your suite, but—"

"I was thinking of my homeworld. This area reminds me of the residential passageways on Bravon. I was having what you call, ah, home illness?"

"Homesickness," Angela answered.

"Yes. That." He placed his hand over hers. In the other hand, he had several fast food takeout bags. In his excitement over talking into an electronic bull, he'd ordered nearly everything on the menu. "I don't know if this is understandable to you, but when I was there, I was excited to get away. I was excited to see fresh air and sunlight. Now, part of me misses the familiarity of it."

"That makes complete sense." Angela stepped closer to him. She liked the contact of his hand on hers. Before she could lift up on her toes to kiss him, one of her neighbors across the hall opened the door. She stepped away from him. "Good evening, Ms. Cunningham."

"Hello." Vin smiled and held out his hand to the neighbor.

"Huh," Ms. Cunningham muttered in return. She eyed Vin, and then his food bags, before shutting her door with a decisive thud.

"Should I have offered her French fries?" Vin asked. "They are delicious."

"No. There's always that one grumpy neighbor, and Ms. Cunningham is mine," Angela said. "She doesn't like me because she thinks I looked at her pet parrot weird in the elevator. If I did, it was because it kept repeating, 'watch out for the po-po, watch out for the po-po,' and making police siren noises. You can ignore her."

Angela gestured that he should enter her apartment. Unlike the lavish hotel suite he'd described in the car, Angela's home was minimally decorated and uncluttered. Photos hung on the walls, most images from her childhood. Her mother was in several of them with her. What little items she had were neatly put away on a bookshelf. The television was old, fatter than the flat screens everyone seemed to have these days. It sat on a plain wood table before a two-seat couch.

"You can put the food on the coffee table." She pointed in front of the couch. "Make yourself comfortable. I'll be right back."

Angela went to her kitchen to grab plates and extra napkins. A tiny thrill of excitement rolled through her. It had been a long time since she'd been on a date.

Angela hadn't been looking for a relationship. She didn't need more complications, but then being with Vin didn't feel complicated. Yes, he was an alien, but for some reason that didn't seem to matter. He felt and looked and sounded human, or humanoid, or whatever they called it. He was infinitely better than the last man she'd been on a date with. That guy had left her with the bill after ordering two lobsters and a steak to take home.

When she went back to the living room, she froze when she saw Vin's clothes piled on the floor. He lounged on her couch, completely naked. Grinning, he held a cheeseburger up to his mouth.

"I see you made yourself comfortable." Her automatic modest response was to glance away, but his posture invited her inspection, and she couldn't help but look. When else would she see a naked alien?

With that in mind, she looked between his legs. Thankfully, that part of him was humanoid in appearance. Actually, his entire body was humanoid in appearance, down to his nicely trimmed beard and his tribal tattoo covering his entire right arm like some bad boy biker.

Vin took a bite of the cheeseburger, and a little ketchup dropped on his chest. He chuckled to himself and swiped it with his finger. "Drive through food."

What was Angela missing? His eyes were metallic. If she acted on the desire flowing through her, would something strange happen? It was hard not to think of all those late night, science fiction movie marathons. Would tentacles grow out of his mouth? Or angry parasitic creatures break out of his stomach? What if she became pregnant with an alien baby and it gestated so fast she was a mother by tomorrow morning?

"Are you sure you're, ah," Angela forced her eyes up to his, "alien?"

He nodded.

"You don't look, ah..." She glanced down his body again and backed up.

"Ah?"

"Like an alien," she finished.

"I don't?"

"Does your skin come off?" she asked, thinking of the skin suit.

"No. Does yours?"

She shook her head in denial. "Do you have strange parts I can't see right now?"

He grinned and glanced down his body. His cock was at full attention. "I'm pretty sure you can see all of me, but I'll be happy to turn around if you would like to see the other side."

Angela began to say that wouldn't be necessary, but then slowly nodded. "Yeah, that might be good."

Vin set the cheeseburger down on the wrapper. He stood and slowly turned, wearing only the shackles. He towered over her. His body looked as if a master craftsman sculpted it. Muscles moved beneath his firm ass, and she bit her bottom lip. Her body reacted favorably to his form. The only difference was three small bumps protruding from one of his hips.

"Ah-ha!" She pointed at the anomaly. "What's that?"

He lightly touched them. "Bravon weather is unforgiving. These glands secrete a natural—I think you would call it a chemical—that regulates body temperature. But," he reached to take her hand and drew it to his hip, "if you rub it like this..."

Vin's breathing deepened in pleasure as her fingers pressed the three bumps and massaged them in tiny circles. Her eyes moved down his stomach to where his erection grew larger. Heat worked its way up her fingers from his skin.

"Now you." He breathed heavily. He stepped closer, but their bodies didn't touch beyond where he held her hand to his hip. "Let me see what you look like."

Angela found herself agreeing. Every inch of her body tingled with anticipation. She lifted her shirt over her head before unzipping her pants. She kicked off her shoes and socks and then pushed her pants and underwear off her hips at the same time. When she stood only in her bra, she reached behind her back to unhook it.

Vin surged forward and pulled her to him. The warm chains bumped against her legs. Her arms were locked to her sides as he wrapped his arms around her. He smelled really good, and she breathed deeply to take him in.

His hands skated over her back. Her breasts pressed into his chest. The lace of her bra offered little protection. A low noise came from him, a completely sexually charged sound of pleasure.

He flicked his tongue along the seam of her mouth. "Damn."

She pulled away. "Why do you keep saying that?"

"Because I'm like an Earth human." He nodded. "And you are damn fine."

Angela chuckled. "Ok, well, damn right back at you."

"Thank you." Vin resumed kissing her. His embrace was passionate, but not rough. His hands molded to her flesh as if embedding themselves over every inch of her soft body. The silver sheen over his brown eyes seemed to swirl and grow in intensity.

Desperate need filled her, and she couldn't stop

MICHELLE M. PILLOW

herself. She didn't want to think or reason. It didn't matter if this was insane. There was an undeniable connection between them, the pull of her body to his as if she recognized him as her mate on a primal level. He was whom she was meant to be with. Logic didn't matter. All the arguments in the world made for time, for taking it slow, for knowing your partner before you jumped in, no longer seemed relevant. None of it mattered.

There was no denying it. She wanted him and was going to have him.

Angela moaned as she pushed against his chest, walking him backward toward the couch. A leisurely smile curled her lips. The electric connection hummed between them.

She straddled his waist, threading her legs under the chains. He leaned over to pull a nipple into his mouth. The material of the bra wet under his kiss and when he leaned away the damp cloth clung to the erect peak.

He pulled her hips, sliding her up until the length of his cock nestled along her sex. She gasped and pushed back. "One second."

"But, I was not finished," he sounded confused as she hurried away. "I can do better."

Angela chuckled as she grabbed a box of

condoms out of her bathroom. Thankfully, they weren't expired. She hurried back. "Safety first."

"Of course, I wish to be safe. Is this place not appropriate?" Vin began to stand, but she pushed him down.

"No, I meant pregnancy protection." She unwrapped the condom and rolled it over his erection.

"Yes, I understand." Vin reached for her, and they resumed where they'd left off.

At first, he didn't penetrate as he glided against her sex. She moaned as she rocked back and forth. His tongue slipped into her mouth as his cock moved between her thighs.

Angela ran her hands over his muscles, exploring the firm ridges of his arms, neck and shoulders beneath her fingertips. She gasped in approval as a small orgasm racked over her. The smell of him, the feel, the look of his body, everything about it consumed her senses.

Vin's eyes met hers as he thrust up. It didn't take long before she was riding him with abandon. His hands molded to her curves as if they learned the way to her fulfillment. It sent her into a state of wild reck-lessness. Just as she was about to explode, he slowed his rhythm and looked deep into her eyes, the metallic orbs appearing as if they could see inside and read the energy of her soul. He cared about how she felt, wanted her to find pleasure, wanted her to be happy.

Without notice, he resumed the determined thrusting that had brought her close. His hands on her hips burned their place in her memory as the flames of their desire rose from the center of her being.

Angela could see in his eyes and feel in the way his body began to tense that his release was coming soon. She wanted it now, but she could tell he wanted to prolong their passion. His will teetered on cruelty and insane bliss until something inside surrendered all control.

Their climax hit them hard, simultaneously enveloping them like a wave in an ocean of ecstasy, cresting and breaking over their trembling bodies, dragging them down into the depths of the wave, only freeing them, once they were completely spent, and close to drowning in the pleasure of each other.

"You are better than ice cream," he whispered.

Angela was too relaxed to respond. She stretched along his body and didn't move from the couch.

Vɪɴ ᴡᴀᴛᴄʜᴇᴅ as Angela slept on his chest. Her weight pressed into him and pinned him down like a comforting blanket. He didn't want to let her go. The soft waves of their energy danced around them, enveloping them in the nearly invisible cocoon.

This moment meant something. He felt that and accepted it for what it was. Angela was his future. Beyond that fact, he didn't have details. She had Connie, and the elderly woman was in no state to go to Bravon. He couldn't take Angela away from her mother, so that left one option. If he wanted Angela, he had to stay on Earth.

Sev would not be pleased.

Sev didn't understand love.

Vin grinned to himself and hugged her closer.

She gave a small, sleepy moan and snuggled against him. Her thigh hit against the chain, and she mumbled, "We have to find a way to get these restraints off."

He heard footsteps coming down the hall beyond her door. "Is someone outside?"

"Probably. The tenants here are up at all hours. Don't worry. Ms. Cunningham, the neighborhood busybody, will be on the job."

There was a brief scream before silence. Angela pushed up, coming instantly awake. They both looked to the door in unison.

"What was—?" Angela's words were interrupted by the loud crash of her front door breaking open.

Vin instantly rolled his body, taking her down to the floor to protect her. He jumped to his feet and faced whoever intruded. A blur of movement entered the small apartment like a swarm of insects, centering around a tall, willowy, dark brown man. He recognized the Galaxy Brides uniforms on the slender alien. What was a Clynder military team doing on Earth? He didn't even bother to hide the fact that he was not from Earth. Vin estimated there were ten of them, but was hard to tell from the number of seedling clone spores gathered along the ceiling.

"Angela, stand up slowly and get behind me," Vin ordered.

"What is that smell?" she asked.

"Stand up," Vin repeated.

"Tracking complete," The slender leader said in the universal star language. Angela made a small, fearful noise, clearly not understanding the garbled words that came from the alien's mouth. "Target has been found."

Seedling spores twinkled like fireflies in the air before falling to the ground in several piles, which then formed into mounds that grew into lighter brown versions of their leader. The longer they stood, the more the planet's oxygen began to react to their skin, changing the color. Once complete the cloned figures from another world moved forward. The Clynder clones' dark eyes had white pinhole pupils that differentiated them from their leader, not to mention their slightly drooping posture.

"Vinglarkenbauer of Bravon, you must come with us," the lead alien said.

"Your buddies aren't looking too well, Clynder," Vin answered, trying to calculate the easiest way to get Angela to safety.

"This planet's toxins do not assimilate well, but they are functioning as they need to," the leader said.

"Do not resist or we will be required to use force. Las Vegas has been determined to be in an unsafe territory. All grooms are required to leave the planet immediately."

"What is he saying?" Angela slowly pushed to her feet behind him and touched his back. He felt her concern. "What's happening, Vin? What are the skinny, zombie-looking alien things doing in my living room? "

Vin hated the fear in her voice. He answered the leader in the Earth language so she could understand him. "I am not going anywhere with you."

Vin didn't recognize the creatures before him, beyond what he'd read. He had not seen Clynders on the ship, and because they wore the uniforms did not mean that they came from Galaxy Brides. There was no way in all of Bravon's fire he was going with them.

He joined his wrist together and grabbed hold of the chains to use them like a weapon. He swung it through the air in warning. "Back away and leave now."

"This territory is compromised," the Clynder stated, finally switching to Earth English. "You are to come with us immediately."

Vin swung the chains again when the clones would come for him, taking an aggressive step forward. He forced the aliens to back up. "I'm staying."

"It is not safe. According to Federation approved contract you signed, we are required to evacuate all grooms from the planet Earth for reevaluation. You and your fellow Killians, along with several of the others, have not fully adhered to Galaxy Alien Mail Order Brides' suggestions for Earth conduct. As a result, the corporation is debating on whether or not to discontinue grooms services, and in the future only offer transport to brides. You were all warned about the dangers of making yourself known to the local population."

"You can't make him leave with you. This is America. We don't operate like that," Angela stated. "He's done nothing wrong. He can stay if he wants to stay."

"I assure you, your government does not operate the way you say," the leader stated. "You will remain quiet."

"I will not!" Angela made a move as if she would push past him. Vin held her back.

"Do you require a reading of the inciting inci- dences, as is your right as an alien client?" Thank- fully, the Clynder did not regard Angela as a legitimate threat, as he focused on his target.

Vin saw several of the clones trying to edge their way along the side of the small room. He snapped his chain in warning and lightly swung it back and forth.

"Yes, he does," Angela answered for him. He saw her reach for a blanket folded over the back of her couch. She pulled it toward her. It would make for a strange weapon.

"Your cousin and your brother destroyed the inside of a casino and interfered with local police business. They made contact with an Earth savant, risking themselves and others in the process. This has aroused the suspicion of other alien-human savants in the area, and they are now crawling all over the strip in Las Vegas looking for alien visitors," the alien leader answered. "The men who chose to arrive as Elvis impersonators banded together and attempted to establish themselves as kings by overthrowing one of the main hotel's governments. They established their reign in the penthouse and demanded tributes. Apparently, they did not realize that 'the king' did not mean the same thing as it does on other planets and that Elvis was not indeed part of the local monarchy."

"Don't tell Mags that," Angela mumbled. Her hand crept along his naked waist, and her fingers pressed into his skin as if indicating he should back up with her. Vin caught sight of her reflection the television and saw she'd wrapped the blanket around her body like a dress. He swung the chains back and forth in a steady rhythm, daring the would-be attackers to step forward so he could smack them with it.

"One groom from Werten tried to kidnap a woman. There are many more incidences that taken by themselves could be overlooked, but as a whole, are not supporting the argument for a sustained trip." Giving what sounded like a sigh, the alien added, "Which brings me to you, Vinglarkenbauer. You were also arrested, and you destroyed your hotel bed, which several of our techs spent hours replicating to replace."

"Gary and Bob chained me to the bed," Vin countered. "What did you expect me to do? Lie there and take it? Have you ever met a Killian?"

"No. You are my first," the alien stated.

"He doesn't understand rhetorical, does he?" Angela again pressed at his side, walking him back a few inches.

"Yes, that word has been uploaded," the alien answered. "However, most damning of all is the fact that images of you have now gone what the natives call viral on Earth communication devices. You have gained infamy as the ice cream criminal. Videos are being made of your videos. I believe there is even a dance version. The Federation monitors are not pleased. What you did is too close to actual Earth-wide exposure."

"Vin?" Angela didn't need to say more. He knew she wanted out of there. "Do something."

Vin began to swing the chains around the top of his head to buy time as he searched for viable options. *"Blendenbut!"*

"What?" Angela asked, confused.

The formed clones began to tremble. The remaining seedlings that floated above them fell to the ground and began to take shape.

"It translates into the Earth word "acclimate" and is a standard intergalactic command for all alien clones to take humanoid form," Vin explained "I read about it in what would be comparable to your magazines. It's a factory default and most forget to disable it."

One by one the slender entities morphed into something more akin to a humanoid form. Their choice of character, however, was not so good.

"Oh, blistersack," Vin swore.

"Evil clowns?" Angela demanded as she cowered

behind Vin. "How the hell is that better than skinny alien zombies? Change them back."

"I can't! That's the only command I remember." He counted more than twenty creatures standing in her small apartment.

One of the clowns began to laugh, a truly eerie sound. Another one waved a puffy glove in the air and gave a psychotic smile.

"Let me guess, all you Clynder-cylinder-slender-whatever things are fans of campy horror movies?" Angela pulled his arm insistently, trying to get him to back away from the threat.

"I do not have that uploaded," the leader answered.

"You haven't fought until you've fought a Killian," Vin shouted at the clowns as he stepped forward and collected the first lot with his chains. Rolling his fists, he combined five heads into one bunch. He twisted the chains, choking all five clowns before yanking to the side to release them.

As the bodies collapsed in a heap, five more stepped forward. Not one to pull the same trick twice, Vin whipped the next lot at their knees and sent them toppling to the ground.

He stepped quickly around the clones on the floor. Vin used the heel of his foot to kill those still alive either by crushing their skulls on the side of the head or hitting them in the throat with one deft blow.

Vin heard sirens and stopped.

"Cops," Angela shouted. She still clutched the blanket around her body to hide her nudity.

"No, thank you. I have this." Vin smiled. He stepped back, realizing that the aliens were now not so forthcoming after seeing what happened to the first lot. The Clynder leader frowned at his fallen clone army.

"I meant the cops are outside. Ms. Cunningham probably called them. They'll be on their way up here. You can't be here with dead clown bodies," Angela stated. "There is no talking our way out of murder. They'll lock you up while they sort it out."

"They're clones. I might have killed their programming, but I didn't really murder anyone," Vin said. Tiny popping noises sounded as the clones exploded into their native nanobot forms. "See."

"Window." Angela pulled Vin. "Hurry. We can take the fire escape."

He wasn't sure where she was going, but he followed her lead. She opened the window.

"Enough." Gary appeared in the doorway. He looked at the disabled clone parts scattered over the floor. To the few left standing, he motioned that they should leave. The Clynder tried to gain Gary's attention, but the shorter man pointed a long arm out of the hall and ordered. "Go. You've done enough damage. I said track him, not hurt him."

"Come on," Angela insisted, ducking under the window frame to step outside. "Vin!"

Vin started to follow Angela.

"There is no reason, Vinglarkenbauer. We can track you by the device in your shackles," Gary stated. "Play time is over. Come with me."

"Vin," Angela insisted.

"Run!" he commanded.

"No, come on. Move your ass, now," she ordered.

"Very well." Gary didn't seem concerned as he held up a small device toward Vin. The shackles on his arms began to beep and grow heavy. His muscles strained to remain upright.

"We can make it, Vin, come on," Angela insisted. He tried to obey but merely stumbled.

When it was all Vin could do to stay standing, Gary made his way forward. "I gave you as much leeway as I could because I know you wanted a chance to be with the Earth woman. Now is the time to make the decision. Do we bring this Angela with us as your bride? Or do we leave her behind? Either way, you have to come with us."

Vin tried to turn around to look at Angela, but the chains restricted his movements. What would she want? But he already knew the answer. She would not want to leave this planet. She would not want to leave her mother. He could not force that decision upon her.

"Can I have a moment to talk to her? Alone?" Vin asked.

"I am apologetic, but time is up. I need your answer." Gary held up an injector. "Transport is coming."

"Angela, I'm sorry," he stated loudly. "I would have liked to have taken the time you requested for a new relationship, but—"

Several humanoid men entered the apartment, cutting off his words.

"Vin?" She sounded like she was trying to come back in the window. Why didn't she run?

"No," Vin stated. "Leave her. She is no threat."

Gary nodded and injected him. His body instantly weakened, and the heavy weight of the chains brought him crashing to the floor.

## 13

Vin was gone. Just like that. Gone.

Angela had never felt so alone and all of her life. The bright colorful lights of the strip, and the buzz of tourists surrounding her, no longer had the familiar appeal that once did. She watched as a little lady with an hourglass figure danced along the path of penny slot machines. At the black jack table, a robust man jumped for joy. She wondered if they were the alien-human savants that Clynder had mentioned. Or perhaps they were the children outside the arcade, left unattended by their parents? Or the waiter paid to sling insults at the guests?

What did any of this matter? They were just games. It was just money. And yet money was so

MICHELLE M. PILLOW

important. She needed it. That's why she was still here working.

Her apartment looked like a tornado had gone through it. The tiny alien clone parts were still on her floor. She left them if only to reminder self that what happened was real. Vin had been there.

And he left her. Just like that. He was gone. Up in outer space.

Angela searched for him as she made her rounds at work. Harris had found an excuse not to partner with her, and she was assigned to her normal shift. The crowds thickened as the hours progressed. They flowed around her, an endless stream of noises and faces.

She saw a tall man walking in the distance and rushed after him. Angela knew it wasn't Vin, but hoped it might have been his cousin or brother. She touched his arm. "Sev?"

"Can I help you?" the man frowned and pulled his arm away from her.

Angela shook her head in denial. "My mistake. Carry on, sir."

The tiny flame of hope inside her died. Her cell phone began to ring and she pulled it from her pocket as she walked away from the man.

"Hello," she answered, distracted.

"Mrs. Borden?" a pleasant voice asked.

"This is Angela." She frowned at the phone, expecting a telemarketer. A group of teenagers began to shove each other and she kept an eye on them.

"This is Mary Hart at Memory Meadows facility. I'm sorry to call so late, but we're having a hard time convincing your mother that it is time for bed. She's clearly tired but she won't get out of her chair. I don't seen anything in her file regarding this behavior, and we were hoping you might come down and reassure her and help her get settled."

"Is she sitting in the chair rocking back and forth with her purse on her lap?" Angela asked.

"Yes," Mary answered.

Angela thought of Vin. "She thinks she's waiting for a bus. Tell her it's time to get off and she can go to sleep."

"Oh, ok, thank you. Sorry to bother you this—"

"Wait." Angela frowned, turning her full attention to the conversation. "Where did you say you were calling from?"

"Memory Meadows, your mother's new care facility," Mary answered.

"My mother is at Sunny Side," Angela corrected. "We haven't moved yet. I don't know who you have there, but it can't be Connie Borden."

Angela couldn't afford for it to be Connie Borden.

"No, I'm looking at her chart right now. She was transferred into our facility this morning by, wait, that name can't be right." Mary paused and she heard the sound of a keyboard. "Oh, I guess it is. My apologies. You'd think I'd be used to Vegas names by now. A Mr. Flame Borden signed her in. He is listed as her son. I assume he is either your brother or husband?"

"Uh, yeah," Angela said, stunned. What was Vin up to? She glanced around the crowd, feeling lost as to what she should do. "Is he there?"

"Here, now?" Mary asked. "Ma'am, it's after hours. Should we have called him first? Your number is the only one in the file."

"But he was there?" Angela began running through the casino, clutching the phone like it was a lifeline.

"Her file says she was dropped off this afternoon. Hold on," Mary's voice became muffled. "Jane, did you see who dropped off Connie Borden today?"

"Oh, honey, those were some handsome boys that woman has," Jane answered. "I might start wearing makeup to work if they visit their mom often. They had fire names—Flame, Fireball, Blaze, something like that. Those boys were handsome and sweet.

They upgraded her care plan and put enough money into their mother's account to cover the next twelve years of monthly expenses. They said they travelled extensively and wanted to make sure she's taken care of."

"Yes, ma'am," Mary returned to the phone. "Flame and a few others were here. They paid the bill in full if that is what you were concerned about."

"Ok, I'm on my way there now." Angela darted through the long hall toward the parking garage.

"Ma'am, you don't have to come. We just had a questions about your mother's routine, and I can try to get her into the bed before you make the trip down."

"It's ok, I should be there." Angela didn't think. Vin had been spotted at Memory Meadows, and she was going to find him.

## 14

Angela ran through the front doors of Memory Meadows and was instantly stopped by security. "Visiting hours are over."

"I'm here to see my mother. Mary called," Angela said. "Her name is Connie Borden."

The man lifted a phone. She glanced around, eager to get past as he verified her information. The front lobby was decorated with silk flowers. Stone tiles formed a star pattern on the floor. The clean, state of the art facility was everything she'd wanted for her mother.

"Sign in here." He handed her a pen and clipboard. "Room 207, down the hall on your right. You can go on back."

Angela rushed down the hall, counting down the

room numbers until she reached her mother's door. She lightly knocked before going inside. Her mother sat next to the bed on her chair. The room had been decorated exactly as she'd had it at the other facility, only there was much more space.

"Mom, hey, it's me." She approached her mother, only to stop when the door opened behind her.

"Hello." She recognized Mary's voice. The nurse stayed a moment until Angela insisted having alone time with her mother. Mary finally agreed, saying, "Since it's her first night, I see no harm."

"It's you," her mother said when the nurse left. She smiled at Angela. "I thought the bus would never come."

"Hey, mom. How are you? Are they treating you well here?" Angela kneeled by her mother's legs.

"Nothing wrong with a hard day's work," her mother answered.

"No, there isn't." She felt slightly guilty about running out on her own job mid-shift. "I had to see you. I had to talk to you. Mom, I need to know something. Today when you moved here remember the guy that came with you and helped you?"

"I always did like that boy." Her mother rocked in her chair holding her purse in her lap.

"Me, too. Do you remember anything about his visit? Did he say anything? Did he...?" Angela's eyes moved toward the dresser. Set on her mother's doily was a fragment from one of the clones. She pushed to her feet and went to look at it. Hope and sorrow filled her at the same time. She'd missed him. Was this his way of saying goodbye? Why hadn't he come back to see her? She reached for it with shaking hands, lifting the doily to see if there was a note or some sign of how she could find him. His name left her on a whisper, "Vin."

"This was the only way I knew to show you how much I care. Earth women like grand gestures. I learned that from watching the rogue transmission waves."

At the sound of his voice, Angela gasped and turned. She rushed to him, throwing her arms around his neck. "How did you escape?"

"I finally read the contract my cousin signed on my behalf." He held her tight and lifted her feet off the floor to keep her against him. "It turns out they had no right to force me back onto the ship if I did not wish to leave. The Federation is not going to be too pleased with that little loophole in the contract. But that is not my problem. Sev was right, Galaxy Alien Mail Order Brides is a questionable organization. They don't seem to care too much about the details of things."

She loosened her hold and he set her on her feet.

"Vin, this is too much. I can't let you pay for this." Angela glanced around the room. At the same time, now that her mom was here, she couldn't send her back. "I'll pay you back."

Her arms rested on his chest. The idea of never seeing him again had filled her with fear and loneliness. Now that he was back in her embrace, she didn't want to let him go.

"I am not worried about money. My brother and I spent about five hours in the casinos to raise the funds. The games are not hard when you can see through the cards. My cousin gave me the idea. He said that humans couldn't see through them like we can, so they think the game is harder. Did you know they took out a tax when you win? They said it was because I am from Canada." Vin shook his head. "I'm not sure that's right. Otherwise this room would have been paid for longer. But it is all right. I will go back to the casinos and win more at a later date."

"Vin, does that mean you are staying here? On Earth?"

"Yes. I would like to." He nodded.

"What about all the radiation you are concerned about?"

"I thought about that. The radiation on this world is no more dangerous than the heat on mine." Vin glanced at her mother when she began to hum to herself, before continuing, "I wanted to show you how much you mean to me, Angela. I wanted to show you how you can depend on me. You said you were worried about moving Connie so I did something about it. We carried all the boxes ourselves, and put the items just the way you had them at the other place. And, because he was worried Sev would cause an intergalactic incident, Gary piloted the moving truck for us. I did not get that pilot upload."

"Drove," Angela corrected in awe. She couldn't believe it. "He drove a truck, not piloted."

Vin frowned. "I'm sorry, but I do not think that is correct."

Angela gave a small laugh at his earnest expression. "Perhaps you're right."

"So you are happy you do not have to lift heavy things? I did well?" Vin looked very proud of himself. "I know women like men to lift heavy objects and reach the tall shelves."

"I think maybe you watch too many rogue transmission waves," Angela teased. "But, yes, thank you.

I do hate moving boxes and carrying heavy things. And I don't use the high shelves because I'm too short. This was the perfect grand gesture."

"So that is a yes? You will marry me?" He made a noise of excitement and lifted her off her feet. Dancing around the room, he hummed a strange song that clashed with her mother's tune.

Angela held on, as she was jostled around. She thought about pointing out that he hadn't actually proposed and she didn't actually accept, but he was so happy and that happiness reflected what she felt deep inside her own soul.

When he finally stopped and set her down so he could gaze lovingly into her eyes, she said, "There are so many thoughts flying through my mind right now, and I can't concentrate on a single one. Are you sure about this? Earth sounds nothing like Bravon."

"I am sure," Vin said without hesitation. "I love you. As long as you will have me, I do not care which planet I live on. Do you think I will make a good Earthling?"

"Well, you are already complaining about taxes. I'd say you're half human already." She leaned in for a kiss, only to stop. "And I love you, too, but there is one condition I must insist upon."

"Anything. I will do anything for you." He nodded.

"Take it easy on the ice cream." Angela didn't give him time to answer as she pressed her lips to his. Nothing beyond this room mattered. She had everything she cared about and she wasn't about to let go. Vin's mouth worked softly against hers as he held her.

"I always did like that boy," her mother said, nodding as she continued to rock on the chair.

## The End

## THE SERIES CONTINUES!

### GALAXY ALIEN MAIL ORDER BRIDES

Spark

Flame

Blaze

Ice

Frost

Snow

**Next in the Series:**
**Blaze**

Sev (aka Blaze) isn't looking for commitment, but there is no way in hell he's letting his brother go to Earth to search for a woman by himself. He's prepared to yank the idiot out of every jail house and ice cream parlor (don't ask) if he has to. It wouldn't be the first time. He can handle a good fight. But what this alpha isn't prepared for was the hardheaded beauty determined to follow him home.

## Prologue Excerpt

*Summer Setting Celebration*
*Frxsolis Settlement, Planet Bravon, Solarus Quadrant*

Sevglarkenbauer watched through the haze of liquor as couples paired up to dance. The old music was the same set of songs he heard every year, and he found comfort in knowing the lyrics before they were sang. There were only a few single women in the settlement, and he had no desire to ask any of them to dance. Instead, he sat with the other ash miners, drinking the stout Killian liquor, and pushing himself into the mind-numbing oblivion that so much alcohol would inevitably bring.

Buried completely underground, the mining settlement of Frxsolis was made up of clusters of decommissioned spaceships and hollowed tunnels.

Solar energy powered the entire settlement. Rows of artificial lights lined the metal rectangle of the commons room where they now celebrated the end of the intense summer season. Long ago, before Bravon's fiery surface had buried the ship's hull beneath a layer of lava and rock, it had been a sky worthy transport vessel. Now, forever entombed beneath the ground, it was the common area of the settlement—a place where they gathered to dine and sometimes, like tonight, for drinking and dancing. As the mining tunnels expanded, they sometimes ran across the ships, which suggested the planet had once been an alien dumping ground for space wreckage. Those were interesting salvage finds.

During the cooler hours, which were still inhabitable on the surface, extendable turbines harnessed the power of the nearby suns to sustain life below by refueling the solar generators. Nearly three thousand Killians lived in Frxsolis. They were a proud, hardworking people. A person had to be to survive in such a harsh environment. Ships had to have special protectant coat even to land on Bravon. For this reason, the only visitors they received were ash haulers. It made the dating pool very, very small.

Sev had gone out several times to maintenance the turbines. Even if he could survive long term on the surface without a protective suit, he wouldn't want to. The suns never set on Bravon, but the light did lessen into a brilliant display of white streaks across the purple and blue heavens. The slick ash sand made it hard to walk, and the desolate charcoal landscape was only broken up by the lava that oozed over the side of the mountain in a fiery waterfall. The bulk of the molten stream sludged into a nearby river, nearly stagnant as it bubbled, sending hot sprays of orange into the air. No living thing survived on the surface, so the only sound was the small clinking noises made by the lava pebbles as they cooled on their way to the ground from the top of the waterfall.

Sev realized he was staring at the ceiling and turned his eyes back to the couples. He took another drink, only to find his cup was empty. He lowered it back to his lap, too drunk to move from his chair. More than likely, he would sleep right where he was.

Ash mining was a hard existence, but they were Killians and Killians never shied away from a challenge. The artificial lights led out of the commons into the maze of tunnels that created the underground settlement's pathways. Several of the corridors still had torches. They weren't really for light so much as a warning system. Sev looked at the fire often. If the flames began to flicker rapidly, it was possible the settlement had been breached, just as it had been the night his parents died when an air lock malfunctioned in the mines. Heat from outside flooded a shaft along the outskirts.

Why was he thinking of that? It had happened so long ago.

He blinked drunkenly, trying to focus his vision on his nearby brother. Vinglarkenbauer yelled more than sang the lyrics of the old song, not bothering to stay on note as his voice joined the others around him. Sev gave a small laugh. Vin was younger than him by several years, and, even though he was now a man, he was still Sev's responsibility.

Sev adjusted is legs and again tried to drink from the empty cup. He grumbled under his breath, this time setting the cup on the table next to him. A figure danced before his view, swaying back and forth. Sev scowled, leaning to look past his cousin, Kalglarkenbauer. Kal danced back in front of his vision and, just as Sev was going to push the annoyance out of the way, Kal handed him another cup filled with solar water to replace the drink he'd just finished.

This gesture automatically changed Sev's drunken annoyance into a welcoming wave. He grinned. "Where have you been? Please tell me Grentakinkensauer didn't trap you in the south tunnels again and try to give you the pointy thumb. Tell me, did she mark you as her own."

Kal shivered dramatically. "I wouldn't dare dream of seducing her away from you."

"She's all yours, cousin," Sev answered. "I want no piece of that crazy."

"Don't you wish we could meet some women who we haven't known since childhood?" Kal sighed wistfully. "It has been too many years since we took extended joint time off from the ash mines, and even longer since we've left the planet. Don't you think it's about time we went somewhere?"

Sev shrugged. Sure, a little female companionship would be a welcome change. "You want to go to the Larceny Casino again? Is Vin even allowed back onboard after last time?"

"I'm not sure. I'd have to check. But I was thinking something a little different." Kal smiled and tapped the device he held close to his chest.

"What do you have there?" Sev nodded to the device as he took a long drink. Sweet slumber was close. "A signature pad? What are you doing with a signature pad?"

"Hey, is that Grenta?" Kal asked. "It looks like she's coming to ask you for a dance."

Sev pushed up in his seat to look around. He felt

a tug at his hand and glanced down to see Kal holding his thumb. The sudden change in position caused his head to swirl and his vision to darken. Just as he was about to ask his cousin what he thought he was doing holding his hand, he felt the blessed numbness of alcohol taking him.

"Don't you worry, Sev. You're going to thank me for this later." Kal's words barely registered as darkness flooded his mind.

MichellePillow.com

# ABOUT THE AUTHOR

## *New York Times* & *USA TODAY* Bestselling Author

Michelle loves to travel and try new things, whether it's a paranormal investigation of an old Vaudeville Theatre or climbing Mayan temples in Belize. She believes life is an adventure fueled by copious amounts of coffee.

Newly relocated to the American South, Michelle is involved in various film and documentary projects with her talented director husband. She is mom to a fantastic artist. And she's managed by a dog and cat who make sure she's meeting her deadlines.

For the most part she can be found wearing pajama pants and working in her office. There may or may not be dancing. It's all part of the creative process.

**Come say hello! Michelle loves talking
with readers on social media!**

www.MichellePillow.com

facebook.com/AuthorMichellePillow

twitter.com/michellepillow

instagram.com/michellempillow

bookbub.com/authors/michelle-m-pillow

goodreads.com/Michelle_Pillow

amazon.com/author/michellepillow

youtube.com/michellepillow

pinterest.com/michellepillow

# COMPLIMENTARY EXCERPTS
## TRY BEFORE YOU BUY!

## Space Lords: His Fire Maiden
## by Michelle M. Pillow

Dev has found a home with a misfit outlaw band of space pirates and he will do anything to protect his makeshift family. He knows he will never be accepted into human society. The demonic race of his birth shuns him and the humans fear him. So when the woman of his dreams comes gunning for his crew, the fiery maiden leaves him no choice but to show just how naughty his demon can be.

## His Fire Maiden Excerpt

*Imperial Palace of the Zhang Dynasty, Planet of Lintian*

"Holy space balls," Rick Hayes swore as he reached forward to poke his finger into the transparent elderly woman floating next to him. The spirit turned and arched her brow in annoyance. When she moved away from him, dark hair streaked with white lifted around her head unhampered by gravity, and her long sleeves drifted in the breeze.

Dev tried not to let his grimace show. It appeared the Imperial Palace was infested with ancestral spirits. Actual ghosts were rare occurrences. In fact, many cultures didn't believe they even existed. He'd seen several milling about though he pretended not to since no one else had indicated they knew the apparitions were there... until Rick's run in with this mysterious elemental lady.

*Blast it all!*

Dev had been on enough high skies adventures to know things generally did not end well when Rick became curious. The pilot's big mouth was sure to drop them into trouble again, and it would be Dev's duty to make sure he pulled them out of it. He owed Rick his life. If Captain Samantha's crew hadn't saved him and made him part of their family, he'd be nothing but a crispy memory told by a Data Moon Base Brimstoneman.

Rarely had he felt such desperation and fear, as he had the day he was almost sacrificed. Bad wiring had compromised Dev's vessel, and his shields had given out during entry into Data Moon Base's atmosphere. The local zealots saw the flaming ball of his ship zipping to the ground near their Earth Settlement and naturally assumed it was a special delivery from the devil.

*Yeah,* Dev thought sarcastically, *because what would be more likely? The legendary devil cared enough to attack a fanatical orb of a dust ball world, or a transporter ship had malfunctioned and had to make an emergency landing?*

Luckily, Dev's Bevlon blood had kept him from burning up during reentry. Not so fortunately, that same blood had also almost gotten him skinned and set on fire. In his nightmares he could still hear a young boy's hateful chanting, *"Into the fire! Into the flame! Burn him now and feel no shame!"*

Dev knew how he appeared to many humanoid cultures. One look and they wanted him dead, all because he had been born Salebinaben Johobik en Dehauberkelsain en Thoraxian en Yyrtolzx Devekin. His father had been full-blooded Bevlon, a demonic-like race in appearance. His mother had been human. The fruition of his parents' strange relationship had produced Dev. It was his red skin and dark eyes that had set the Data Moon zealots off. He'd inherited the intense coloring, large body size, and black eyes and hair from his father. The humanlike form he'd received from his mother.

*"Burn him! Listen to the angel and burn the demon spawn!"*

*"Crucify him!"*

*"Burn the demon!"*

The voices were etched deep into his memory. Dev hadn't expected to be rescued. Back then, no one cared whether he lived or died. Bevlons did not coddle their children into adulthood, and he didn't know his human mother.

His loyalty to Rick and the others was from more than the fact they'd saved him, an outsider no one else cared about. The crew had become something Dev had never imagined he would have—a real family. Sure, Rick was like the pesky little brother he sometimes wanted to throw into deep space without a suit, but no one else better try it.

Remembering the past helped Dev stay focused in the present, but more importantly it reminded him why he wasn't dragging Rick from the palace by his hair. Rick made another move toward the spirit. Dev focused a glare of warning in the man's direction and gave a small shake of his head. Rick winked back at him.

Dev had been alone until Captain Samantha and her band of misfits came for him, a condemned stranger. Crewman and empath Evan Cormier had seen Dev in one of his visions. Rick, Samantha, and Evan had come in with laser pistols blasting while the brothers, Lucien and Viktor, had waited with the ship ready to make their getaway.

Dev would give his life to protect his makeshift family. They accepted him, teased him, baited him, and, yes, occasionally called him Barbecue Boy, but they would put themselves on the line to save him. Together they traveled from adventure to adventure, wherever their ship landed. Recently, Samantha had married a cat-shifter and was now settled on the man's home planet of Qurilixen. It did not change their bond, and Dev would always answer her call if she needed him.

His new captain, Jarek, was Samantha's brother-by-marriage. The man had offered them a place on his ship. He needed to replenish his dwindled crew, and they needed a purpose. Jarek and his men were all honorable, even if they were borderline space pirates.

Jarek's second-in-command, Lochlann, was a dragon-shifter. The men came from the same home planet. The two were long-time friends who had run away from home because dragon-shifters and cat-shifters were at war. Neither one of them had wanted to fight, so they chose the high skies. Though the war on Qurilixen was over, the men's families didn't fully accept their friendship.

Lastly, there was Jackson, a highly trained super soldier. To Dev, the man was a kindred spirit. He had the same drive and determination, and the almost compulsive need to train for battle in the Virtual Reality room aboard their ship.

This was Dev's life. It was more than a half-demon reject could have ever hoped to achieve. He did not dare aspire to have more. And it was how he found himself in a royal alien palace silently praying Rick would not sexually proposition an old lady's ghost.

One would think escorting Princess Mei to visit her family wouldn't demand a quick departure off planet. Then again, *One* wouldn't know Rick's penchant for mischief in any situation.

They stood inside the Hall of Infinite Wisdom

located in the center of the palace compound. The building was a large structure, set high upon stone to tower over the surrounding courtyard and gardens. If the ornate décor was any indication, the local royals had lived in isolation for some time, away from any kind of real intergalactic conflict.

Dev stayed toward the back of those gathered to keep an eye on everyone. He didn't like their odds of escape from inside the belly of the fortified palace, but bad odds didn't mean impossible. There were numerous official reasons why they had come to the planet, but really it was so Jarek could ask for Mei's parents' blessing to marry her. Since, technically, the crew had kidnapped Mei to begin with, it wasn't likely her parents would be too excited by the proposal.

Evan crossed his arms over his chest and kept his attention on the Emperor and Empress. Dev wasn't sure if Evan was trying to read the royals, or trying not to, so he watched the man for a sign that all was not well. Evan did not like using his ability, but would if necessity called for it. Returning a kidnapped princess to angry parents with an army at their fingertips might warrant such a necessity.

Like a child with a new toy, Rick couldn't seem

to help himself. He ran his hand into the apparition's upper leg. "She feels like air."

Mei turned at Rick's words and eyed the situation. She nodded toward the spirit, and quickly introduced, "This is my great-grandmother, Zhang An. She is my ancestor who helps to watch over and guide us," before continuing her somewhat private conversation with her parents and Jarek.

Rick made a move to touch An again and the spirit silently glided out of his reach. An was clearly aware of what was happening but chose to ignore Rick as she focused on her living relatives. Dev let loose a captured breath as it appeared the crisis might be averted.

Dev shared a quick look with Jackson. The man leaned toward him and whispered, "Should we grab Rick before he does something really foolish?"

"Next time I vote we lock him on board the ship." Dev studied the locals, trying to judge their temperament. He had a feeling one word from the Emperor would produce a significant number of trained guards. Part of him wanted the fight. It might be a fun challenge. Then again, he wouldn't want to put the others in harm's way.

"Mei belongs with the captain," Jackson whispered. "If they don't approve, we take her by force.

Look at how they act toward her and then watch her expression. She does not belong here. If only we would be so lucky to find—"

"Jackson, you have to feel her," Rick interrupted softly. He had stepped close to the spirit once more. "I swear, it's like she's not even there, but she is."

Jackson made a move to grab Rick as if he'd forcibly pull him from the room. Dev placed his hand on his arm to stop him. "This is the captain's future. Let him handle it how he sees fit." Observing a servant looking into the room from a doorway across the hall, Dev nodded to direct Jackson's attention to her.

"If Rick's ass gets thrown into a local prison for feeling up a dead woman, I'm not going after him." Jackson kept an eye on the servant until she disappeared. Dev knew it was a lie. Jackson would be the first one to volunteer for the mission.

As Mei began to argue about her future happiness with the ancestral spirit and her parents, Dev felt sorry for Jarek. Dev couldn't imagine having a woman to love. He long ago accepted he was not meant for such things. After years of being ridiculed and feared as a demon, he was used to people trying to attack him without reason or provocation. What sane woman would want a half-breed devil in her bed, let alone in her heart? If the Emperor thought Jarek was unworthy of his daughter, Dev could only imagine what would have happened had a demon stood in the captain's place.

"She should marry the father of her unborn child," An declared in support of Mei leaving with Jarek.

That caught Dev's attention. Mei was pregnant out of wedlock? Her parents didn't seem too pleased by the news. They stared at the couple in shock. The Emperor looked ready to call his guards.

"Oh, blasted spaceholes," Jackson swore. His entire body tensed. "Get ready."

Dev waited, carefully watching the Emperor for a sign of attack.

"Way to go, Cap!" Rick yelled suddenly, breaking the awkward silence as he drew the heated attention toward himself. "You sent off some straight shooters right up the ole—"

"Rick," Dev growled, unable to take the man's nonsense a second longer. He grabbed him to shut him up.

"Ow, let go," Rick demanded. "*I* didn't knock her up."

Dev released him, realizing a second too late that Rick knew exactly what he was doing. The man only acted the way he did to pull negative attention away from the captain and his pregnant lover. In comparison to Rick, Jarek would look like an exceptional choice. Also, if everyone was staring at Rick, the lovers would be able to make a run for it if they so chose.

The ploy worked. An turned on Rick to keep the attention off Mei and Jarek. "You insolent little..."

"Whoa, easy there, ghostly sweetness, you'll get your chance at me," Rick said, grinning at the older woman. "No need to call Dev names."

The bad joke was Rick's attempt to defuse the situation he'd created. An's figure shuddered with light and her face tinted with pink. Furious, she pointed at him, "I will teach you respect, little man. You will bow in the presence of my greatness."

Rick paled, apparently realizing that he'd played his asinine role too well. "Hey, now, I was just joking around. Things were getting a little tense, and I was just trying to save the captain from everyone's anger. You know, lightening the mood with humor."

"Do not make me curse you," An warned.

"Rick, I'd listen to her and say no more," Evan interjected.

"Easy, don't get your, uh, gown in a twist," Rick said, ignoring Evan's sensible advice. Though he was great at causing trouble, he wasn't the best at calming it. "No need to threaten us with whatever mojo power thing you have."

Jackson hit Rick's arm. "Shut your black hole."

"Ah, so you think you are funny?" An's eyes glazed with white. "Let's see how humorous you and your friends think my power is."

Jarek started to take a step forward to protect his men. Dev awaited his command. Mei pulled Jarek back, shaking her head. "She predicts their future. No physical harm will come to them."

An's voice took on an ominous quality. "Together you travel, and together you'll remain. Tied and joined like the five elements of our people. The road to happiness is very rocky for all of you."

"What does that mean?" Lochlann whispered. It was the first he'd spoken since they'd walked into the palace hall.

"Is she telling the truth?" Jackson questioned Evan, as if skeptical of the ghost's powers.

"I don't know," Evan answered. "I can't read spirits."

"Great going, space cadet." Jackson nudged Rick.

An's eyes cleared, and she smiled vindictively, evidently knowing something they didn't. "You will find your love hidden within the mystery of the five elements. One element for each of you." She moved her eyes over Lochlann, Evan, Dev, Jackson, and Rick. "The corresponding element will hold the secret to your future happiness. But fate is not clear. If you do not recognize it, you will lose it and be forever alone."

"Elements?" Lochlann repeated. "What elements?"

"Yes. The secret of your future is hidden in the five elements—metal, water, wood, earth, and fire."

"Which one am I?" Jackson asked.

"And I?" Lochlann questioned.

"That is for you to figure out." With that, An blew away on a sudden gust of wind. Dev watched her leave the hall. Seeing her ineloquently saunter away when she thought the living could no longer see her did take away some of her scary mystery vibe.

"How does predicting what will come curse us?" Rick frowned.

"She just gives us enough to consume our thoughts," Evan said. "Trust me, knowing only a very small piece of something will drive you mad. The thought will creep into our heads and make us crazy."

"Metal, wood..." Lochlann tried to recite.

"Water, earth, fire," Evan finished.

"Dev's got fire, that's easy," Rick said. "And I must be metal because my body is rock hard with muscles."

"I think the elements refer to the ones we are meant for," Evan said. "Not who we are."

"She didn't say that," Rick protested. "I'm metal. I know it."

Dev didn't speak. There was nothing for him to say. It was as if she'd found the one secret weapon that could hurt him and stabbed him with it—the desire to be loved and accepted. A physical ache filled his chest, so he held himself rigid and waited for the pain to pass. He knew he was not meant to find love, but to have it dangled before him so unexpectedly was most brutal. His hand clenched. He wanted to punch Rick. He wanted to chase after An and make her tell him more. For if he had a chance at losing love, then that meant there was actually a chance he would someday find it. That hope was the cruelest part of all.

And maybe the whole curse thing was just a mean prank told by a cranky spirit, and nothing had really changed.

www.MichellePillow.com

## Space Lords Series

His Frost Maiden

His Fire Maiden

His Metal Maiden

His Earth Maiden

His Woodland Maiden

## PLEASE LEAVE A REVIEW

### THANK YOU FOR READING!

Please take a moment to share your thoughts by reviewing this book.

Be sure to check out Michelle's other titles at www.MichellePillow.com